DULL PENCIL ANTHOLOGY

of YA short fiction
by hitherto unknown writers

Volume 1

DULL PENCIL PRESS

2014

DULL PENCIL PRESS

www.dullpencil.com

First published in 2014 by
Dull Pencil Press

Dull Pencil Anthology
of YA Short Fiction By Hitherto
Unknown Writers, Vol. 1

ISBN 978-0-69236741-4

Editor-in-Chief
Poem Kim

Editors
Christabel Abbott
Bethany Glass
Michelle Kim
Trevor Wrightson

Cover design by Geraldine Lau

Publisher's Note
Stories contained in this book are works of fiction.
Any resemblance to actual persons, events, businesses,
institutions, or locations are entirely coincidental.

Printed in the United States of America

EDITING CREDITS

POEM KIM
Co-Founder, Editor-in-Chief
is a high school student in Northern California

CHRISTABEL ABBOTT
Co-Founder, Editor
is a high school student in Northern California

BETHANY GLASS
Editor
is a college student in New Haven, Connecticut

MICHELLE KIM
Editor
is a high school student in Northern California

TREVOR WRIGHTSON
Editor
is a college student in Oxford, England

CONTENTS

Dark Side of the Moon

Cybil Fierst

*is a college student in New York City
who grew up in Mississippi*

When I lived with my mother, whenever I spoke, she told me gently, and rather eloquently, that I might give some consideration to keeping my mouth shut because nothing worthwhile ever seemed to come out of it. That's probably why, around the age of ten, I stopped speaking altogether.

It did wonders for our relationship. She made me brownies for dinner every night and even invited me to watch reruns of *CSI: Special Victims Unit* with her before sending me off to bed. Of course, there were some difficulties at school and with the few friends I had prior to the event. But those were soon resolved through placement into the school's special education program, and finding new friends there who seemed to genuinely appreciate my outstanding listening skills.

When I started high school, someone there decided that something about me was amiss. Maybe it was the slight limp in my stride. Or it could have been that someone had heard me singing *Eclipse* by Pink Floyd, as I always did during lunch break while sitting on the toilet. New York City's very competent Child Protection Services was contacted and I was examined by a physician and a psychiatrist. They determined that some of my bones had been repeatedly broken when I was very young. This could not be true since I had no memory of such things. They also concluded that I had no physical or neurological reasons for not being able to speak. This was true, but I couldn't understand why that should have surprised anyone.

So, it was that I was sent to live with my father; a father I did not know existed, and who happened to live in a town named Succotash (affectionately called Tash by its residents), in the state of Mississippi.

It turned out my existence was news to him too.

"Your mother and I met while I was in law school in New York," he explained, a potent Black Mississippi twang in his molasses slow words. "She was a waitress at a diner I frequented during the two years I was there. We were friendly and I walked her to her place one night when I happened to still be around at closing time. She invited me up for a drink and one thing led to another. In the morning, as I was leaving, she threatened to tell the police that I had raped her unless I continued to see her. I freaked out. You know, where I'm from, Black men sometimes still get lynched for stuff like that. I dropped out of school and came back home to Mississippi as fast as I could, and finished up my studies here.

"Apparently, your mother had hired a private detective to track me down, so she knew where I was, but had never followed through on her threat and had never contacted me to tell me about you. It wasn't until those social workers showed up to take you away that she shared my whereabouts with anyone.

"And… well, I guess that just about sums it up. I hope I didn't upset you, but I believe that knowing the truth is important."

I nodded, as if I approved of all that was said.

"To be honest with you, when they contacted me and sent me your picture, I didn't believe that I could be your father. You looked as White as a White person could possibly be. In fact, you're paler than any White person I've ever met, and I could not see anything of myself in you. Not in your violet blue eyes, and certainly not in your golden hair. And I think those social workers were more skeptical than I was, asking me to provide blood samples for a paternity test. In any case, I'm a firm believer in science, and those tests don't lie. You are my daughter, and I mean to do right by you. Okay?"

I nodded again, saddened that my father was a firm believer in science.

———————————

We lived in a one room trailer home, the most common kind of habitable abode in Tash. My bed was a lovely green polyester sofa that produced jets of dust which erupted into the air no matter how softly I sat on it. The kitchen sink was next to the sofa, and its leaky faucet dripped fat droplets onto an unwashed skillet which always resided in the basin, and was like a lullaby that coaxed me to sleep every night. When there was wind, the entire trailer would gently roll, giving the illusion that our home was in motion on a bumpy highway, on our way to an exotic destination. "Wait until hurricane season," father said, "That's when it really gets fun."

After he got his law degree in Jackson, father went about trying to realize his dream of *empowering* the Black people of Mississippi. It was a dream borne out of his wish to eradicate "The illusion of inferiority that burdens every Black person in Mississippi as soon as they're born."

He explained that, in Mississippi, Blacks were like sheep and Whites were like herding dogs. Just one dog could intimidate and corral a hundred sheep. "A consequence of centuries of brainwashing of Black folks, that they don't know what they're doing and need White folks to tell them what's right and what's wrong," he offered. "That's why there has been no statewide elected Black official in Mississippi since the Reconstruction, despite the fact that Blacks make up almost 40% of the population.

"I was under the same spell when I was a young boy," father continued, as he sighed in disbelief of his own past ignorance, "but I woke up when my high school English teacher, this powerful Black woman, showed me how I was smarter and more capable than any of the White kids in my class. She encouraged me to go to college, something no one else ever said was even possible for someone like me, and give my life meaning by helping to give voice to our people."

He believed that Blacks in Mississippi could not "wake up" until they started empowering themselves by electing Black politicians who will represent their interests in the state's power structure. "First, we have to start in towns and cities," he said. "You have places all over Mississippi where the people are mostly Black but the mayor and all the people in power are White. Even when a Black candidate runs, most of the Black folks vote for the White guy."

After working for the past ten years at a law firm as their "token Black" associate, father had saved enough money to support himself indefinitely, as long as he lived *very* modestly, while he conducted his crusade.

"Of course, I didn't expect to have you in the picture," he smiled, "but we'll make it work."

His first target was his hometown of Tash. It had a miniscule population of just over 200 people, 150 of them Black. However, the town has had a White mayor for as long as anyone could remember. In fact, no Black person had ever even run for mayor in the more than 150 years of its existence. The current one had been in office for the past thirty years, and was the owner of the town's only grocery store. A position of great influence, considering half the townspeople brought their groceries on credit while waiting for their monthly food stamp allowances. So, father moved into his childhood trailer home, which was his mother's sole asset of any value and which she left to him when she passed away five years ago, and have been busy for the last three months going door to door trying to convince his neighbors to vote for a Black candidate in the upcoming election. He persuaded his childhood friend, the town's only auto mechanic, whom everyone seemed to trust, to run for the office and to make the rounds with him.

When I arrived, election was only a month away, in August, and there were only fifteen people who had committed to voting for father's friend. It didn't look good, considering that all of the thirty or so eligible Whites were expected to turn out and vote for the incumbent. Since school was out for the summer, and being concerned that my lack of speech might point to something more serious, he took me with him as he made his last push to mobilize the Black Tash'ians.

At the town's Baptist church, father and his friend made speeches imploring the congregation to open their eyes and to take their futures into their own hands. It was an impressive sermon that called upon the spirits of Martin Luther King, Malcolm X, Nelson Mandela, and even Marvin Gaye, to please "bless" the cowardly Black souls of Tash to shed their slave mentality and grow backbones to stand up for themselves. Unfortunately, the churchgoers weren't very attentive, and seemed more interested in my identity and what I was doing there. Seated in the front row, next to the reverend and his wife, I could feel the hundred pair of eyes that were focused on the back of my head.

The old lady sitting behind me finally posed the question that was on everyone's minds. "That's all fine and dandy," she rasped, with one of her white gloved hands gently resting on my shoulder. "Now, who is this sweet White angel who came in with you?"

Father hesitated, perhaps uncertain as to the consequence of his answer. "She's my... little girl... my daughter." His eyes reddened as he spoke. An overwhelming warmth of being wanted by, and belong with, someone came over me, and I realized that I hadn't previously experienced such a feeling.

An uncomfortably long silence was followed by a ruckus of words that seemed to generally convey delighted surprise, and I even heard a "hallelujah" amongst the chorus. When the service ended, many of the congregants came up the pews to take a closer look at me. After some time, with unanswered greetings and questions hanging in the air, it became clear to them that I did not speak.

"Oh, she's dumb, ain't she?" proposed one portly man, who was wearing a freshly ironed striped suit, but with a farm worker's boots.

"No, no… she just… chooses not to talk," answered my father, who took hold of my hand and gently squeezed it, as if to let me know that folks here weren't very sophisticated and meant no harm by calling me dumb. I squeezed back, to let him know that I understood.

"Well, I can believe that," said a high pitched voiced middle aged woman with a fake bird on her bonnet, who may have been the man's wife. "Too many folks like you talkin' too much nonsense," she mocked, pointing a livid finger at the man, "It's no wonder I haven't stopped talkin' myself!"

People slowly started to ask father about the up-coming election, asking questions like, "What difference does it make in a shit-hole town like this?" and "What if the mayor gets sore for losin' and stops givin' folks store credit?" Father and his friend spent the next hour an-swering their questions, and re-assuring them that only good things could come from people taking hold of their own destinies.

Father and his friend were excited and energized when we were alone in the church parking lot, sensing a turning of the tide. As we walked back home, father re-marked, "I think you're my good luck charm. I'm not sure exactly why, but I think you're the missing piece in this puzzle."

On election day, the three of us stood outside the courthouse, where the ballots were being cast and counted, greeting and shaking everyone's hands. The Whites avoided getting too close to us, though many stared longer than they should have, with quizzical wrinkles on their foreheads. The Sheriff came by at one point, commenting that "many" of the voters were con-cerned that I was standing with two men who weren't my relations, and wanted him to check to make sure I was ok. When father explained to him that I was his daughter, the Sheriff raised his eyebrows.

"Is that right?" he said, shifting his right hand so that it touched the revolver on his belt and tilting his head so far back that I could see the follicles in his nostrils. "Is that right Miss? *This* is your father?"

I nodded and hooked my arm into father's arm.

"Alright, alright, didn't mean nothin' by it," the sheriff said, while backing away with his hands raised in front of him. "Y'all have a good day now."

"I remember him from high school," father said, when the sheriff had gone back into the courthouse, "He used to have this old pickup truck with a Confederate flag spread on the hood, and a black colored mannequin noosed on the rear. He would drive around, dragging that thing into the Black part of town while wearing his daddy's Ku Klux Klan hood. What really gets to me now is that no one did anything about it, including me. We all just looked away in fear and locked ourselves away in our home. It was like we were ashamed that someone had noticed that we were Black."

The sheriff soon re-emerged from the building, this time with the judge who was overseeing the ballot counting. With the current mayor and his supporters on one side of the steps and us, and several of father's friend's relatives, on the other, the judge proclaimed, "It looks like we've got ourselves a new mayor."

The now former mayor and his entourage looked stunned. Father and his friend quietly shook hands, big smiles on their faces, and the new mayor turned to his relatives to partake in a grand group hug. Father walked over to the judge who looked like he was consoling the former mayor, and chatted with them briefly before returning.

"Unbelievable," he said, "they're claiming that the race was close, and that almost half of the hundred people who voted had voted for the old mayor. That just isn't possible. I'm positive that all seventy Black voters had voted for our guy. Goes to show that the only way we can win is to win so big that they can't possibly deny it."

As we were walking home, father recounted his memories of his English teacher, and how he was sure she would be proud of him. "'To give voice to those who had none', that's what she thought was the most worthwhile thing to do with one's life. You know, come to think of it, she actually never specifically said Black people. I must have just assumed that's what she meant. But knowing her, she probably did mean exactly what she said, that we need to do what we can to help all voices be heard."

"This is good," I said.

Father stopped and turned to look at me, his mouth agape. He slowly closed his mouth, the corners turning up as it did so.

"Yes. Yes, this is good," he agreed.

El Juramento (The Promise)

Salvador Jimenez

*attended schools in Southern California
and currently works in Latin America*

Today was supposed to be the biggest day of Roque's life. Today was the day he was supposed to become somebody; somebody to be respected and feared, not just another Mexican teenage perdedor trying to survive in East LA. But he didn't care about any of that. He had a more important, a more personal, reason for wanting to become a member of El Unión

The iniciación would not be easy, sometimes the aspirante died, he was told. If you cried or begged to stop, you were out. Not just that, they would take all your clothes so that you would have to walk home in naked shame. And you were forced to walk through the main residential roads because they would drag you off and beat you again if you tried to hide. Roque thought he was ready; not many could have withstood the daily beatings he used to get from his father, an alcoholic day laborer. He had also been secretly training at Victor's Mixed Martial Arts gym, in Long Beach, more than two hours of walking and bus rides away from his neighborhood. Far enough that no Unión eyes would see him.

Victor, the gym's namesake and owner, had told him to go away when Roque showed up two years ago, asking to be trained but with no money to pay for it.

Desperate, Roque had confided in Victor the purpose of his quest, and Victor, after lengthy rumination, had agreed. Though Victor was born here, his parents and older siblings were illegals like Roque's family, and he remembered well their stories of victimization when they first arrived – when they were most vulnerable. He could easily empathize with Roque's mission. However, Victor quickly saw that Roque had considerable natural abilities and was saddened by the idea that it should be wasted only to serve a personal vendetta.

"You have real talent and could become professional one day," Victor advised Roque on the day before the iniciación, "Do what you have to do, but promise me that you will come back."

The idea of becoming a professional fighter, of beating others and being beaten by them for money, disgusted him. Roque had no intentions of coming back to the gym after the iniciación, but he didn't want to disappoint Victor who had been so kind to him.

"I will," he lied to Victor.

———————————————

The abandoned warehouse where El Unión's iniciacións were held was gutted, with its bare, skeletal concrete surfaces spray painted with territorial markings and names of distinguished former members. The floor was remarkably clean, to prevent an initiant from picking debris up off the ground to use as a weapon. It was also coated with epoxy, making cleanup of blood – evidence, if someone died – relatively easy.

"Why don't you be a good niña and go home to your mother? Why do you want to put yourself through this?" Juan Soto, the líder, asked impatiently. His words boomed and echoed as it bounced around the walls and made their way up towards the blown out windows near the ceiling.

"Because I want to be somebody and live like a man!" Roque screamed, trying to summon more courage.

The six senior members of El Unión moved around Roque, until they had surrounded him in a wide circle. Each of them would get three minutes to do their worst, with Juan Soto dishing out the last test. To pass, you didn't have to beat any of them; you just had to survive the beating they gave and not give up. But Roque's intention wasn't to just survive; he needed to beat Juan Soto. And in order to do that he had to either kill him, make him unconscious, or have him beg for mercy, an almost impossible feat considering Juan's fighting prowess and his considerable pride.

Roque had to be careful. He needed to allow the first five to beat him, so as not to raise Juan's suspicion. But he had to carefully manage the amount of punishment he received, to preserve enough strength and sense to defeat Juan… to keep the promise.

The first four were easy. Roque held his elbows close to his ears while keeping his chin close to his chest, so that his arms would absorb the more powerful side punches they threw. He also positioned his torso so that punches and kicks to the body impacted at an angle. After each of their three minutes, they huffed and puffed in exhaustion while Roque groaned, pretending to be in pain.

His fifth opponent, Marco Ramirez, was smarter. He was the oldest member of El Unión and Juan's trusted lieutenant. He was thirty five years old and had been a Unión since he was fourteen. Though only five and a half feet tall, he looked like a linebacker whose face had passed through a string curtain of razor blades. The most prominent scar ran diagonally across, from his left temple to the right jaw line just below the ear. Everyone respected Marco and he could have been the líder but gave it to Juan, after Juan saved his life by jumping in front him and taking a bullet shot by a rival gang during a drive by.

"You know what you're doing chico," Marco said. "You don't fool me," he continued, "and I know you got something up your sleeves."

Rather than trying to punch him standing up, Marco grabbed Roque's legs, lifted him up, and slammed him down onto the concrete floor. He pinned Roque on the chest with his left knee and pried Roque's left arm away from his face and hammered him with powerful blows that took Roque to the edge of unconsciousness.

"Tell me what you're up to," Marco kept repeating, shouting the demand into Roque's ear between punches. Roque had to do something or he was going to pass out, and all the years of hard work and planning he'd put in for this moment would have been for nothing.

Roque quickly wrapped his arms and legs tightly around Marco's torso, like a terrified baby chimp clinging to its mother while she swung on branches to move between trees. Marco was befuddled by Roque's move, but continued to throw jackhammer punches to the left side of Roque's face while trying to pry him off with his left hand. But the shorter distance to the face and the awkward position took away much of the sting.

"I'm not your mother chico and there's no milk for you there," Marco said, trying to embarrass Roque into releasing his embrace. When that didn't work, Marco became frustrated and ran toward a sharp bend in one of the concrete walls while shouting, "You're loco but I'm más loco, and now you're going to die!"

There was no choice. Roque released his hold and fell to the floor.

"You're still going to die," Marco declared, as he grabbed Roque by the neck and wound back his fist. However, the timer rang, signaling the end of Marco's three minutes. His eyes were ablaze with rage and Marco seriously considered ignoring the rules and delivering his death blow. He thought better of it though, knowing that it would be a stain against his honor. He released his grip on Roque's neck but spat on him before turning away.

"He's up to something," Marco warned Juan, "You might want to stop the iniciación."

"We can't do that," Juan replied, a bit surprised by Marco's suggestion, "I can see that the kid has some skills, but he's no threat to me. Don't worry. I'll finish what you started. He won't make it out of here."

Roque's left eye was grotesquely swollen and had completely shut. There was no way he could prevail over Juan in an extended match with only one eye. He had to put him down fast. Otherwise, it was over.

"Ok niña, now it's our turn," Juan mocked, as he approached Roque from the left, his blind side. Roque had to be patient. He needed to wait and hope that Juan would throw a punch rather than attempt a takedown like Marco. And he couldn't react or turn his head until the punch landed on his face.

As soon as he felt the impact, Roque turned and lunged toward Juan, and grabbed his right arm with both hands before Juan could retract it. Juan tried to pull his arm away, shifting his shoulder and body to the right. Roque leapt and secured the back of his left leg behind Juan's neck, above the arm. As Juan bent over to try to get free from the leg, Roque leapt again, this time landing the back of his right leg on Juan's back, below the arm. The off-centered full weight of Roque on his back caused Juan to fall over, his face now on the ground. Roque had succeeded in engaging Juan in an arm-bar position, a powerful mixed martial arts submission move that he had practiced a million times at Victor's studio, where the victim's arm runs across his chest, pulled by his opponent between his legs. It was an incredibly painful hold that can be used to easily break or dislocate the arm, though the victim almost always submitted before that happened.

"Beg for mercy Juan, and I will let you go."

Roque bent and pulled Juan's arm, enough to cause excruciating pain but not enough to break it. Juan gritted his teeth but did not let even a grunt escape his mouth.

"Go to hell niña!"

"You will be the one to go to hell monstruo!" Roque's rage, never verbalized until this moment, flowed out of him like water behind a broken dam. "You don't remember me? You were supposed to help us get to the city after crossing the border. Instead, you robbed my family and took away my sister. When you returned her, throwing her to us like she was garbage, she was almost dead. She couldn't live with the memories of what you did to her, and before she finally killed herself, I promised her that I would make you pay; that I would make sure you and your gang would never do such things to any more good people. And I will now keep my promise!"

Roque pulled harder and Juan groaned loudly, unable to contain the pain any longer.

"Beg for mercy!"

"No!"

Thirty seconds left.

Roque knew that he couldn't pull or bend any harder without breaking Juan's arm, but he had to. Juan was too tough to beg unless he was out of his mind with pain. Roque bent Juan's arm near the elbow, snapping the bone at an unnatural angle. Juan screamed in unholy agony.

Some member of El Unión moved in, unable to control their impulse to stop the mutilation of their leader. But Marco signaled to them to step back. He knew that the only way Juan could save himself, and El Unión, would be for him to bear the punishment without quitting. If he failed, they were finished.

Fifteen seconds left.

Roque pulled until the arm popped out of its socket at the shoulder. Juan screamed again, and continued to do so as Roque rotated the arm around in circles, grating the bones.

"I do not wish to kill you. I am not an animal like you. But you must beg or I will kill you!"

Five seconds left.

"Mercy… mercy, por favor," Juan groaned.

Roque immediately released the hold, just as the timer rang. He felt as if an oppressive weight had been lifted off of him. His emotions were overwhelmed, and he briefly sobbed, his eyes buried in his knees.

Roque got up and faced Marco and the others.

"No more El Unión. No joining another gang or starting a new one. That is my first and last order as the new líder of El Unión. On your honor, all of you must abide."

Marco initially looked defiant, his jaws clenched tight. He let out a long sigh, and finally said, "Understood, and we will abide. I will see to that."

Roque turned toward the warehouse door. Juan was still face down on the floor, perhaps unconscious from the ordeal. He was an empty shell now. Word would spread.

It was done.

And now life for Roque could start.

Aethon and the Cave

Eliza D.

*was in the eighth grade when she wrote this story
and is currently a high school freshman*

Aethon opened his eyes and groaned.

"Where am I?" he muttered to himself. He pushed himself up from the sand, brushing his dark brown hair away from his blue eyes. His wet clothes clung to his skin. Wet clothes? When had he gotten wet? And where did all the sand come from?

"He's alive!" Aethon heard a woman cry.

"Of course I'm alive," he said thickly, blinking rapidly, his eyes adjusting to the bright sun. "Unless this is the Underworld…"

He peered around. Surrounding him was a small village of simple huts. The people were wearing plain clothing that smelled of sheep. An old man wearing a dark brown cloak hobbled over to him. The old man had a long white beard and no hair on his head, and had crooked teeth that allowed his tongue to poke through the gaps.

Nope, this is most definitely not the Underworld.

"You…" The old man paused to cough. "You are on the island of Andreusson! The Cursed Island of Poseidon, the Sinking Island!" he stated melodramatically, although his wheezing slightly ruined the effect. "I am Areoles, the medicine man of Andreusson; father of

Aridides. And who are you?" Aethon opened his mouth, and then shut it. "Now, don't be shy and tell us your name! It's not like a god has cursed you," Areoles paused and his eyes narrowed, "or are you?"

"No…" said Aethon slowly. He wasn't sure he could trust these people, but he also didn't want to be kicked off this island. Besides, this island was cursed by Poseidon; what harm would it do if he were cursed by Poseidon too? "They call me Aethon," he told Areoles.

Tired and hungry, Aethon sat on a small wooden stool in a large sheep skin tent belonging to Areoles.

"So, Aethon, eh?" asked Areoles, filling a bowl with foul looking porridge that he was cooking over a fire for the two of them. He had invited Aethon to stay with him and his son while Aethon looked for a job and a permanent home on the island. According to the villagers, there was no way off the island, unless you wanted to risk being eaten by sea monsters.

"Yeah."

"You look like you've been through a war," he observed as he handed Aethon the bowl.

Aethon stared at the lumpy porridge in his hands. "You could say that."

"Oh? What do you mean?"

Aethon sighed. Would this old man ever shut up? "That's really none of your business."

"As a host, I would ignore that statement and change the subject," wheezed an amused Areoles. "But as a stubborn old man, I would prefer it if you'd tell me all about it."

Aethon sighed again, louder this time. "I'm sorry, I'd rather not."

But the old man had one last question: "Why are you here and not home with your family?"

Aethon stiffened. "I don't have one anymore."

Areoles gasped and awkwardly walked over to Aethon, offering another bowl of the suspicious looking porridge, apparently unaware of the fact that Aethon hadn't yet touched the first bowl.

A horrible scream reverberated through the village. Both Aethon and Areoles left the hut to make their way to the village square where the scream had emanated.

Before they reached it, they could see a young man with impossibly tangled blonde hair collapsed in the center of the square. A look of horror crossed the old man's face. "Aridides?" Areoles wailed. "My son, what has happened to you?"

Despite his old age and his wobbly gait, Areoles was surprisingly fast. Aethon had to sprint to catch up. "Aridides!" he wailed once more. "What has happened to you, my dear Aridides?" Aethon peered over Areoles' shoulder and gasped. Aridides' face was covered in a disturbing mixture of mud and blood. Even with the gunk on his face, Aethon could still tell that Aridides was a handsome, fit youth of perhaps 16 years old, just a few years younger than himself. A shepherd ran over to the growing congregation of villagers around Aridides, panting. "I saw him stumbling down the hill and screaming his head off. He came from the direction of… of…," He dropped his voice down to a whisper, "the Cave."

"The Cave?" an old woman repeated, eyes wide. "Are you sure?"

"What's the Cave?" questioned Aethon. The shepherd turned around to face him. A chill ran up Aethon's spine. Was he seeing things, or was he looking at… himself?

"The Cave is… um, why are you staring at me?"

"I… I… you… me… uh, um… he, I mean, you look like… me." Aethon choked out. The dark brown hair, the slightly pointed nose... It was like looking at himself-except his mirror image had brown eyes.

Pericles' eyes widened. "Now that I think about it, you do look like me. You could be my long lost twin!"

"What?" spluttered a shocked Aethon, "I don't have a twin brother; my family is dead!"

"How about right now we pay less attention to your speculations, and more to the fact that *my son is dying!*" Aridides shrieked, trying to stop the blood trickling from his son's side.

"Yes, of course," said the shepherd Aethon-look-alike, adding: "Sorry."

"Pericles, what did you say Aridides was doing?" asked Areoles.

"Well, he came through the sheep's meadow screaming: 'It's horrible!' and then he fell. I reached for his hand and pulled him up and asked him if he was okay, but he ran down this hill, clutching his side."

Areoles kneeled down beside Aridides, checking for any sign of a wound. He paled, and removed Aridides' hand from his side. There was a huge burn wound and a deep cut that anyone could tell was fatal. Then Aridides choked out his final words: "The Hypnocide... Cave…" His eyes glazed over.

"Aridides?" cried Areoles, looking broken. "My boy, my poor, poor boy!"

"I believe he said something about a Hypnocide and a Cave," said Aethon. He turned to his "twin" and asked, "What's the Hypnocide?"

Pericles stared at him. "You really don't know what the Hypnocide is?" Aethon shook his head. Though Pericles was obviously shaken by Aridides' death, he took a deep breath and explained, "The Hypnocide is the legendary monster who guards this island. It drags it beneath the waters after a century, and pushes it back up after another century."

"Wait, this island sinks beneath the waters? Then how do you survive?" asked Aethon.

Areoles stared at his son and said, "We don't." Aethon was horrified. "Poseidon told our ancestors that only a man born on this island but raised on another could kill the Hypnocide and release us from its grip. And you, Aethon, was born on this island like your brother Pericles." He motioned at his mirror image. "I knew it the moment I saw you. I was so happy that the gods had finally answered my prayers by sending you back here. I told them I would give up anything to save this island. And so they have delivered you and in turn have taken my precious Aridides away from me as payment."

Aethon stared at him. "I wasn't born on this island. I'm no hero; and I certainly didn't kill your son."

Areoles looked very disappointed. "If you defeat the monster, you save our island. It must be you. Many of our bravest men have tried, but Poseidon stated that it had to be a man raised on another island. And it's not easy – defeating the Hypnocide is not only physical, but also mental. And we have only twenty-four hours before this island sinks once more, so I suggest you make your decision right now," said Areoles.

Aethon shut his eyes and thought for a while. *These people will die if you don't at least try to help... But then I will die! But won't I die anyway when the island sinks? Who am I kidding? I've never fought a monster before... Then again, I could at least try, make up for what I did back home... And it could count as revenge on Poseidon...*

Aethon opened his eyes, a sick feeling in his stomach. "I- I must be crazy... but I'll try."

I can't believe what I'm doing.

"Hey! Aethon!" shouted a young man. Aethon turned around to see Pericles running up the grassy hill towards him.

"Yes?"

"Oh, okay. So, I'm Pericles, you know, your twin," he panted. He was now right in front of Aethon, wearing a baggy, light brown tunic and carrying a sheepskin bag. "I want to help."

"Yep, yeah, sure," said Aethon distractedly, trying to walk away as quickly as he could, his own sheepskin bag swinging. Inside was a crudely shaped sword that would have to do (seeing as it was the only one on the island), a water container, and bits of dried sheep meat (just in case) – a gift from Areoles.

"Look, I want to go with you!"

"What? Why?" Aethon said, flabbergasted.

"Well, why not?" questioned Pericles. "Aridides was my best friend," he said seriously. "I want to avenge him." He thought for a moment. "Plus it could give us time to get to know each other," he added. "And I'll tell you how we were separated."

"It's too dangerous," Aethon said flatly.

"I want to help," Pericles insisted. "You know you can't do it alone."

Aethon could see that Pericles would never give up, and they were losing time arguing. "Fine," Aethon sighed. "You can come. But I'm not to blame if you die," he added, eyeing the shepherd warily.

Pericles nodded his thanks, humoring Aethon. What difference did it make if he dies fighting the Hypnocide or when the island sank?

"Come on," Aethon grunted. They set off towards the Cave, crossing through the fields that smelled of fresh manure.

"So," said Pericles, almost tripping over a pile of sheep dung. "Whoops. I'm fine. So you're my twin. I always knew I had a brother," continued Pericles. "Did you?"

"No."

"So, where are you from?" asked Pericles.

"A different island."

"Where?"

"Ways away."

"Oh. Why are you here?" questioned Pericles.

Aethon realized it wasn't just the old men (AKA: Areoles) who yapped too much on Andreusson. It was *all* of them!

"I don't want to talk about it," Aethon snapped.

About half an hour of walking passed without a sound. Not a peep came out of either twin's mouth. They approached a hill with a dark tunnel at its apex – the Cave. "Whoa," murmured Pericles. It was pretty impressive for a cave; there were stalactites and stalagmites hanging from the ceiling and jutting up from the floor, and a low wind could be heard blowing through the cave.

"This must be it. I guess I'll go first. Remember, stay close to me unless you want to be eaten or ripped to shreds," ordered Aethon, gulping down his fear. "Always keep your torch lit. If you see any movements, tell me." They both entered the Cave, torches lit and held high.

The flames from the torches made eerie, flickering shadows on the Cave's walls. The chirps of bats made frightening echoes as they bounced off the walls. Pericles looked nervously over his shoulders, while Aethon attempted to peer ahead.

When Aethon finally reached the Cave's main chamber, he stopped to rest. Luckily, he played discus a lot back home, and was not as unfit as Pericles, who was drenched in sweat and lying on the Cave floor. The strange heat emanating from the Cave's walls certainly didn't help though.

Pericles attempted to start another conversation. "Would you like to hear the story of how Mother and Father died?"

Aethon shrugged. He never knew his biological parents – in fact, he had always thought the people who raised him *were* his biological parents, until the fire.

Pericles decided to tell Aethon anyways, to kill the uncomfortable silence. "Eighteen years ago, Father was watching the sheep while Mother was cooking dinner. She was pregnant with both of us at the time. When Father returned home, Mother told him that we were coming, and to get the village healer as quickly as he could." Pericles paused for breath. "Father rushed through town until he found his sister, our aunt, who was the healer before Areoles. But Mother didn't survive giving birth to the two of us. Father blamed his sister, and forced her to leave the island. What he didn't know was that she had taken you with her, because you reminded her of Mother. See, you've got her blue eyes. That's the only difference between us." Pericles paused to check Aethon's eyes, which were in fact blue. His own eyes were a golden brown. "She wrote that she took you with her in a note that she left behind in our home. Father was devastated, and wasted away soon after." Pericles looked away from Aethon. "I was raised by a farmer and his wife, but they're gone too," he said, his voice cracking. "We had assumed you were dead, killed by the sea monsters. I thought I had no family...until today." Pericles gave Aethon a hopeful smile.

Aethon was silent, drinking in the story he had just been told. "I lost my adoptive family too," he said softly. "And it was my fault." Aethon cleared his throat and began his tale, feeling he owed it to Pericles.

Aethon threw a discus to his friend, Cadmus. Cadmus caught it, and threw it back. "Hey, Aethon!" he called. "Why don't we find somewhere else to play?"

Aethon raised an eyebrow. "Now why would we want to do that?"

"Too crowded!" he called with a grin.

It was true – the two of them were playing in the town square, where many scholars gathered to talk about government and philosophy.

"All right," Aethon agreed. "Why don't we head to the Pillar?"

The Pillar was as the name implied: a pillar. But this Pillar was made entirely of marble and stood high into the sky. The Greek letters painted in gold on its length dedicated the Pillar to Poseidon, in hopes of improving their fishing season. The Pillar had stood atop the hill looking over their island for centuries.

Cadmus linked arms with Aethon and said. "Why not?"

As the two best friends joked and talked with each other, they soon found themselves at the bottom of the hill. "Okay," said Cadmus. "This is a good enough spot." But after twenty minutes of discus throwing, Cadmus suggested they head home.

"No way!" said Aethon with a laugh. "This is too much fun! Let me throw once more, and then we'll go home."

Cadmus shrugged. "Fine."

Aethon threw the discus, but a wind blew it off course and it landed on top of the hill. "I'll get it," Aethon said dragging himself up the steep hill. When he made it to the top, he found the discus – but the Pillar had a new crack in it and was threatening to tumble over. Aethon froze, then moved as quickly and as lightly as he could to pick up the discus. But the discus was right in front of the Pillar, and Aethon's arm brushed it as he picked the discus from the ground. The Pillar toppled over and hit the ground, shaking it. Immediately, a storm brewed.

Rain poured harder and harder, flooding the city. The strange thing was – the water was salty. Aethon felt a chill as he realized that the storm must be the work of Poseidon, and that he was responsible. "You are correct, mortal," a voice boomed around Aethon. "Because you destroyed my Pillar, your island shall pay – your family especially. You and your bloodline shall be cursed, and the people who adopted you..." In the distance, he saw a house catch on fire. "...shall not survive."

Aethon paled, backing away. From what, he wasn't sure. He felt his foot fall down upon nothing, a single thought passing through his mind before he fell:

My family is going to die, and I can't do anything about it.

"...When I awoke, I found myself here, on this island." Aethon finished. "My family only consisted of my adoptive (though I thought they were my true) parents, who were the most kind and loving people. I don't know what happened to our aunt."

Pericles nodded, and there was a silence between the two. "Perhaps we could get some rest now," Aethon suggested half-heartedly.

Pericles spread out two sheep skins and two wool blankets that he had brought with him. They settled in, and Pericles was out quickly. Aethon took longer to fall asleep. As much as he wished that Pericles was his brother and that he still had a family, he couldn't help but feel skeptical.

Aethon woke up after a few hours, only to find that Pericles was gone. "Pericles?" called Aethon uncertainly. "Pericles?" There was no answer. Then the cave shook and there was a huge blast of air forcing him out of the main chamber. But as soon as it stopped, the tunnel flipped. Aethon had to grab onto one of the small knobs of rock to keep from falling down one of the other small chambers. The rock felt slimy and squishy. But normal rocks weren't slimy and squishy… Then another huge blast of air shot him straight up and out of the tunnel. One second he was seeing stalactites and stalagmites, and in the next he felt the earth colliding with his face. Or did his face collide with the earth? Well, either way, it *hurt.*

He heard the screech of an angry eagle, and the screaming of… *Pericles*? Looking up, Aethon saw that there was no Cave, just a giant monster that he assumed was the Hypnocide. What had Aridides said? *The Hypnocide… Cave…*

The Hypnocide is the Cave!

"AAAHH!" screamed Pericles from behind a large boulder. What Aethon guessed was the Hypnocide, screeched a mind numbing shriek that felt like a million fingernails gliding down his back. It was an enormous snake with the head of a jaguar, and one hundred razor sharp claws like a mutated centipede with eagle claws for legs. Though he was shaking in fear, Aethon's instincts took over. Instincts… he didn't realize he had any until now. He got up and hacked and jabbed at the monster with the sword he'd brought along and the monster bled inky black blood and shrieked. The Hypnocide tried in vain to grab him with its claws, but Aethon moved with uncanny speed to evade its clutches, surprising the Hynocide, not to mention Aethon himself. But all of a sudden Aethon felt helplessly compelled to look into the monster's glowing red eyes. As soon as he looked into them, he couldn't look away. It was as if the Hypnocide had trapped him with its gaze, each passing second taking Aethon deeper into a spell that seemed to systematically shut down his brain. Pericles shouted at him to look away and harshly jerked Aethon until the pupils of his eyes shrank back to their normal size and seemed to refocus back into reality.

Aethon, adrenaline pumping through his veins once more, took another swing at the Hypnocide, chopping one of its many claws off. But once again he felt an uncontrollable urge to look at its eyes, and once more Pericles shouted and ran towards Aethon to break the spell. The Hypnocide whipped its attention to Pericles, roared, turned, and lunged at him, grabbing Pericles with one of its mighty claws. Pericles stopped screaming. In turning itself around, however, the Hypnocide revealed its unprotected belly, which Aethon promptly stabbed then sliced along the length, releasing a torrent of ink black blood that flooded the hillside. The huge monster screeched one last time, writhed, squirmed, and finally laid still.

"Pericles!" Aethon shouted. "Where are you?" There was no answer. "Pericles?" he whispered uncertainly. He looked frantically over the Hypnocide, searching for Pericles in its long and scaly body. Then he saw him, lying in one of the claws, a giant stab wound on his chest from one of the talons. Aethon tugged him out onto the soft green grass. "Pericles? Pericles? Are you alright?"

Aethon began to despair. It seemed as if he had lost his entire family. His parents, the people who raised him, and now the brother he had only known for less than a day. Salty rain began to fall. Aethon glared at the sky. "Why have you taken everything from me? My family, my home... what more do you want?"

"I am impressed," boomed Poseidon's deep voice. "It seems I have misjudged you. I was sure you would fail, being a mortal… but here you are."

"How?" Aethon asked, surprised that Poseidon actually responded to his complaint. "If you were so sure I would fail, why did I not?"

After a lengthy silence, Poseidon answered, "There was a prophesy from Apollo that decreed a man born of this island but raised on another would one day slay my beloved Hypnocide. Of course, I took all possible measures to ensure this never happened.

"But, I believe my brother Zeus, who has always been jealous of the glorious creatures in my oceans, gave you a blessing of reflexes worthy of the gods. I should have known, since that day many years ago when you escaped my sea monsters."

Aethon was upset by the revelation. "You tried to have me killed as a mere child?"

"Well, you've destroyed my Pillar and now my prized pet, the Hypnocide. Let us call it even and move on, shall we?"

"No, I think that is hardly fair," Aethon protested, though he knew Poseidon could strike him down in a second.

The rain fell harder.

"And what do you proposed I do in return for this… *injustice*?" Poseidon rumbled impatiently.

"Bring back Pericles. He's the only family I have left. Please, I beg you!"

After a long pause, Poseidon let out a long and mighty sigh. With that, the rain lifted. Aethon understood that he had "won".

"Aethon?" It was Pericles.

Tears flowed from Aethon's eyes. "I'm here. We defeated the Hypnocide and saved the island."

Pericles sat up, groggy. "I dreamt that there was a man in a hood. He wanted payment to cross a river..." He blinked his eyes. "Strange."

Aethon was overjoyed, and pulled Pericles into a deep hug.

"I'm so glad," the hero choked.

Pericles patted him awkwardly on the back. "Me too, brother. Me too."

Second Chance Night

Reini Lin

is a high school student in Northern California

I don't belong here.

The thought pounds ceaselessly in my head, beating out a rhythm I can hear even over the deafening music.

Actually, in hindsight, I really don't know how Damien managed to convince me to come in the first place. This isn't exactly my scene – but it sure as heck is his. I cast a glance over to where he's surrounded by his usual crowd of admirers consisting of girls who want to date him and guys who want to *be* him.

I, on the other hand, am standing next to the refreshments, sipping my third cup of root beer. Completely alone, save for the bored-looking junior refilling the jugs of beverages. Probably here for the volunteer hours.

At least *she* has a reason to be here.

I bite back a sigh and look down into my drink, half-hoping to find some sort of deep meaning in it. The only thing I see is the bottom of my cup.

Tossing the empty plastic cup into the trash, I start to maneuver my way across the room, pushing past people I vaguely recall from elementary school and keeping to the walls for the clearest path to the exit. For a moment, I think I hear Damien call my name – but no, it can't be. *Why would he care? He's having the time of his life. It's senior prom, for Christ's sake.*

Clearly, we don't have the same interests. It's actually kind of amazing how different two people can be. It's also kind of amazing that we're best friends.

But still, he's never really understood me completely.

Not like – not like *she* used to.

Quickly, I push the thought away before it can fester into something unpleasant. Remembering does nothing but drive the knife deeper.

Finally reaching to door, I step outside the room, away from the mass of bodies, away from the stifling heat that makes it hurt to breathe, away from the chaos and noise. Inhaling deeply, I turn, waiting for my eyes to adjust to the sudden darkness – and nearly choke in surprise.

Someone's already there.

She's perched on the edge of the bench, like a scared bird ready to fly away at any moment. The brief flash of light escaping from the still-closing door illuminates her painfully familiar pale blonde hair that I ache to run my hands through. Bright sea-green eyes lock onto mine, and I can feel something in me shatter again.

Pain flares in my chest, hot and overwhelming. For a moment, my good judgment lapses, and I'm seized by the sudden urge to run to her, to take her in my arms, to hold her close the way I've done a thousand times.

But then I remember.

Reality crashes into me. I'm acutely aware of the bile rising steadily in my throat, of my heart thundering irregularly against my thoughts of *No, no, no* –

"Wait," she whispers.

I am frozen. For some odd reason, my limbs have decided not to obey me.

"You're Lucas." It's a statement, not a question. And *oh, God, her voice is just as angelic and beautiful as I remembered.*

I lose the ability to speak. To breathe.

She tilts her head a fraction and turns the full brilliance of her gaze onto me. "There were pictures of you and me in my room. From... before."

My chest is on fire, my stomach hurts, my lungs don't seem to be working, and still I somehow manage to speak. "Yes." My voice is steadier than I would've thought, even as my gaze flits from my shaking hands to the stone tiling beneath me to the stars above.

Anywhere, anywhere, anywhere but here.

"You were my boyfriend, weren't you?" Her eyes roam my face, desperately searching for answers.

The question hangs between us, an elephantine object.

I cannot speak. I only nod, once, and hope she sees me in the shadows of the building.

"I knew it." There is a pause. Then, almost resentfully, she murmurs, "They never tell me the important things. Only the happy, useless things." I can only assume the "they" are her mother and older sister. We've never had a good relationship, but then *it* happened, and ruined any semblance of one. I wasn't even allowed to visit her in the hospital.

It only makes sense that they'd never told her about me.

"What do you want to know?" The question leaves my lips, unbidden.

She responds immediately. "Everything. What you liked about me, what you hated about me. What my pet peeves were. I don't know, everything."

The words start slowly, cautiously. "You... you bite your lip when you're trying not to smile." I try to swallow, to no avail. "When you write, you tuck your hair behind your ear with your little finger. I love that." Distantly, I smile. "You hate horror movies but love romances with tragic endings. You made me sit through dozens of those."

The sound that escapes me is somewhere between a hysterical laugh and a choked sob, and then everything comes rushing out, faster and faster.

"You hate being called 'baby' as a term of endearment. You make a point to drop pennies on sidewalks. For little kids to find. You always listen to music with one earbud in. You… you were the best thing that ever happened to me."

I chance a glance at her and see something like a sad smile play across her lips. "You loved me." It isn't lost on me that she uses past tense.

The breath whooshes out of me, sharp and ragged against my throat as it claws its way to freedom.

She smiles, faintly. "I'll always be outdone by my old self."

I start to argue – *of course not, how could you think that* – but then stop. Loathe as I am to admit it, her words do ring true – all I think of when I see her is the ghost of who she used to be.

The thought makes my stomach twist.

"Let's start over," she says suddenly, looking up at me with a little smile quirking her mouth as she puts out her hand. "Hi, I'm Eden. I just lost my memory in a car accident, so life is a little weird. It's prom night, and I have no date. And you?"

For a moment, silence reigns. Then the tips of my lips curve upward as I take her hand – and *oh, it feels so right* – and pull her up. "I'm Lucas, but you already know that. I'm likewise dateless, and I believe in second chances."

prologue to the novel

Castoff

Travis Darcy

is a teacher in the San Francisco Bay Area

From the lost scrolls of Torlach,

High Mage, Kingdom Daire:

All girls conceived in King Daire's quest for an heir are tossed away like rubbish. None are given true names, but share the common name,

Castoff.

It was ill luck for a mother to hold a dead child. But this one would travel to the Otherworld in a few more breaths. What harm would it do to let her carry the dead infant along? The midwife placed the naked, blue-skinned babe on the mother's chest.

"Rejoice," the mother murmured. "The child is born."

The midwife snorted and busied herself wringing out bloody rags in a bowl of dirty water. Who in the wide world rejoiced the stillbirth of a girl child—a lowly Castoff? No doubt the mother already had one foot in the Otherworld, speaking shadow words that held no meaning for the living.

Suddenly, a tiny fist clawed the air. The lifeless baby pinkened. With a small cough it began to cry.

"Give this to my daughter," the woman whispered,

clutching a silver locket at her neck. "And tell the mage she has come."

The midwife hobbled to the bed, the silver drawing her like a leech to blood. "I will. I promise." The lie soured her mouth. She spat and shrugged off her unease. Falsehood might darken her fortune, but silver would certainly brighten the days to come. Who would know? The mother was one of the Travelers. She had no kin in the castle to weep her loss or lay claim to her possessions. The only witnesses in the room were the babe and the bastard boy sleeping on the cot in the corner.

By the time the midwife had unclasped the silver chain and slipped the locket into her pocket, the mother was dead. The child's cries, however, had grown lusty, as if strengthened by the last of her mother's spirit. The midwife sighed. She had not bothered with swaddling. Why waste cloth on a dead baby? But now it seemed the child would live.

"You'll find no milk there, Castoff." The midwife lifted the wailing infant from her mother's cold breast and shuffled to the table where she had laid two swaddling cloths in preparation for the birth—woolen for a girl, fine linen for a boy. Had the child been a boy, the king would have tossed her a silver coin. But the fates had not been altogether unkind. The locket would fetch a fine price at market. The midwife's mouth watered. She would buy soft bread and yellow cheese and eat like the fat kitchen folk for a month.

After wrapping the babe tight in the coarse woolen cloth and placing her in the roughhewn cradle that served as first bed for all Castoffs, the midwife turned to the corner to awaken the bastard boy. She was startled to find him sitting up and eyeing her coldly. Had he witnessed her thievery?

"Aedan," she snapped. "Go tell your royal father it is only another Castoff born this night."

"Go tell the king yourself, old woman." The boy rose from the cot and strolled towards her.

The midwife's face reddened. "You have not passed the mage's test yet," she sputtered. "You are only a bastard. I am your elder. You have no authority over me."

The boy had not even seen his seventh nameday. Yet the darkness in his eyes iced her blood. The midwife stumbled away from him, until her back pressed against the hard unyielding stones of the wall.

"The test will reveal what the stars already know. I

shall be *Prince* Aedan," the boy grinned.

For a moment the midwife relaxed. It was all a jest. He was only a child, after all. But then the black of his pupils spread to the whites of his eyes, like ink spilled on parchment. The eyes pulled her down, down into a dark abyss that seemed to stretch forever.

The midwife clutched her throat. She tried to scream, but her breath fled the darkness. Her heart froze. Her mind fractured. The boy smiled and sucked the life from her like mother's milk.

The last thing the midwife felt before following the dead mother to the Otherworld was Aedan's hand slipping into her pocket, pulling the silver locket from it.

excerpt from the novel

Chronicles of Aradia

Madison Fisher

recently graduated from college in Austin, Texas

Having two horns sticking out of her head really made things complicated. She was born that way, a victim of nature's roll of the dice; at least that's what Rochelle Adelestein had always assumed. Her mom told Rochelle that she looked into getting them surgically removed when she was an infant but all the doctors she went to said it couldn't be done. There were critical parts of her brain matter that looped inside and were fused with the horns, they explained, and she would die instantly if they were removed. They were like conjoined twins, the horns and Rochelle, their fates intertwined forever.

It was bad enough that Rochelle was the only Jewish kid, *and* the only one with a single parent, at her high school in Dallas, Texas, the Bible belt's buckle, it would be a complete disaster if anyone were to find out she had horns. Luckily, she also had very thick hair, and as long as she rolled it up into a bun, there was no way anyone could see or even feel them.

That was, until they started to grow.

It was unmistakable. One day they were well hidden under her puffed up hairdo and the next morning, the tips of the horns slightly, but clearly, broke the surface.

The night before, she went outside to take a look at the new star in the night sky. It was a supernova, according to all the news on television and the internet, thousands of light years from Earth. She remembered thinking it seemed to her that the star was directly above her. After a few minutes of gazing, she developed a sharp headache, near her horns. She now wondered if the headache had anything to do with her horns' sudden growth.

"What am I going to do?" Rochelle screamed in horror to her mom. "I can't go to school like this!"

"Oh, I don't think anyone will notice," her mom replied dismissively, and with a hint of a smirk at the corners of her mouth.

Has this woman finally gone senile? Rochelle thought, *Does she not, like, have eyes?*

While Rochelle tried to re-do her hair to better conceal the horns, her mom was on her cell phone, whispering and giggling.

"Mom, seriously, are you not even going to help me here? Don't you care that my life is ruined?!" Rochelle pleaded, furious at her mom's nonchalant attitude.

Her mom murmured something into the phone then hung up. "You know sweetheart, you don't have to go to school if you don't want to," she offered, as she approached her.

Rochelle couldn't believe her ears. *Was this the same woman who bragged to everyone about my perfect attendance record since kindergarten, and once forced me to go to school with a 102 degree fever?*

"Really?" Rochelle replied, incredulous, "But what if I miss something important?" *Now I sound just like her. How brainwashed and lame am I?* she wondered in dismay.

"Oh, I don't think it's so important anymore," her mom assured her.

"Anymore"? What does that mean? This is weird, Rochelle thought. *Oh well. School sucks, so whatever*.

She spent the rest of the day experimenting with her hair, trying to figure out ways to camouflage and safeguard the horns against every possibility. *Some joker was bound to try to mess with it*, she reasoned. She finally settled on a complicated arrangement that required two dozen pins and clips. She could have achieved the same result with just a dozen, but she knew that having redundancy and backups were critical in such life and death situations.

Next morning, Rochelle got up an hour early so that she could re-construct her hair. After she washed and blow dried it, and as she was heating up her curling irons in the bathroom, her mom opened the door.

"Mom, please, like I've asked you a million times to knock first."

"What are you doing?"

"Duh. What does it look like I'm doing," Rochelle replied, tired of the mundane exchange, "I'm getting ready for school."

"Well, that might not be a good idea. Why don't you stay home today too?"

"What? Why is that not a good idea? Mom, you keep talking in riddles and I can't figure out what's going on here! Do you know something that I don't?" Rochelle was so upset at this point that tears welled up in her eyes.

"Oh sweetheart, I'm so sorry," her mom consoled, worry lines creasing the forehead between her brows, "I know I'm being kind of…cagey. Some people are coming by here today. Some experts on this type of thing. They'll clear this whole thing up… one way or another."

Experts? One way or another? Does she mean doctors? Are they going to tell me that I'm going to die?

Countless anxiety ridden thoughts raced through Rochelle's brain. And she was getting that headache again, the same pain around her horns that she had felt two nights before while looking up at the new star. She placed her hands on top of the horns to try to soothe the area and noticed that the horns seemed a bit longer than when she last touched them last while washing her hair.

"They're getting even bigger!" Rochelle shrieked, "Oh my god, oh my god, oh my god…," she repeated, while she walked briskly in circles around her mom, and with her hands over the horns.

"Don't panic Rochelle," a deep baritone voice that sounded like Darth Vader boomed and reverberated in the hallway where she and her mom stood. The front door to their house was open, and three men, dressed in black suits and sunglasses, stood on the foyer, adjacent to the hallway's entrance.

"Oh, you've come just in time!" Rochelle's mom said, clearly relieved to see the men. Her mom took hold of her hand and led Rochelle toward the living room, and pointed and gestured to them to meet them there.

The men, who looked like agents from *The Matrix*, sat themselves on the lavender colored love seat sofa, the only seating available in the living room, crammed together along its short span. Rochelle and her mom brought over the foldable metal chairs from the adjacent dining area that normally served as their seats for the small laminate dining table. They never had guests, so it wasn't until that moment that Rochelle was struck by how transient their home seemed. How their furnishings were a mish-mash of highly standardized, mismatched pieces that you might find in basements of churches, army barracks, or town halls. Everything was portable and foldable, built for quick re-arrangements and easy storage. Her bed was a cot with a thin twin mattress. Her desk was a laminate platform, identical to the dining table, with foldable metal legs that were anodized in neutral grey. Her *closet* had wheels and was enclosed with canvas and a zipper. Only the sofa, upon which the men were seated, had any aura of permanence. But it was something they had lugged in from the curb when their next door neighbor abandoned it there when they moved away a few years ago.

Rochelle was brought out of her meditative thoughts when the man in the middle finally spoke. "So, let's do the introductions, shall we?"

"Yes," her mom replied, "As you all know, this is Rochelle. Rochelle, these men are from… uh… our church."

"Church? *Our* church? What are you talking about mom? We've never been to a church. We're Jewish for God's sake! Or at least that's what you always told me. We've never even been to a synagogue!"

Her mom was clearly distraught by Rochelle's outburst. She swallowed hard and fidgeted in her seat. "I know that's what I told you sweetheart. It was to… protect you. These men are here to help me set things straight."

"That's right," the man in the middle confirmed, "We had to all be sure before you were told. And now that your horns are growing, and the new star has lit up directly above you, we are sure."

"Sure of what?" Rochelle asked with a whiny crack in her voice, as she mentally tried to prepare herself for what she suspected was some sort of dire medical diagnosis.

"You are Aradia, our savior."

"Huh? What? What kind of disease is that?" Rochelle asked, confused.

"No, it's not a disease. You are Aradia," the man in the middle repeated, as if he expected Rochelle to understand the significance of his declaration.

"Let me try to elaborate," the man sitting to his right offered, his words saturated by a Slavic accent that was hard to place exactly. He was older than the other two, had white stubbles that were unevenly long in the folds of his wrinkled face, and had gold front teeth that reflected too much light. When he took off his glasses, Rochelle could see that his eyes had red pupils.

Rochelle gasped, taken aback by the eyes.

"I apologize. This must all be very puzzling and frightening for you. I am Lazlo, the grand Warlock of the order of Aradia. Basically, we are witches. You, as my comrade has told you, are Aradia, the prophesied savior of our people.

"To put it simply," Lazlo continued, "you are to us who Jesus is to Christians."

excerpt from the novel

Greenville High

Myles Gunji-Jardine

is a high school student in Spain

The Concise Oxford English Dictionary collided with the back of my head, propelling my nose into the hard wooden desk. There was an audible crack and I heard the kids around me wince.

"MARTIN! HOW MANY TIMES HAVE I TOLD YOU NOT TO FALL ASLEEP IN MY CLASS?"

Dazed, I rubbed the back of my head and squinted at the corner of the white board where my name was printed in large, aggressive capitals.

"Fourteen…?" I ventured.

The book swung around for another thwack at my head and I saw sparks.

"Eighteen," said Dr. Farnworth, adding another line to the already impressive tally.

"I told you to get your eyes checked, didn't I?" he said menacingly as he walked back toward my desk.

"Didn't I…?"

I braced myself for the dictionary again (Farnworth's weapon of choice for as long as I had been taking his English Literature class) but the bell rang and the classroom burst into a flood of chair-scraping, allowing me to escape.

Two weeks after the official start of autumn, Mother Nature sent a heat-wave across the country so that the dead leaves on the ground crunched pleasantly under foot and the flowers started blooming again. Summer was extended.

Unfortunately, school doesn't stop for heat-waves, and although we had been repeatedly warned about it, somehow I had managed to forget about the math test that morning. To make matters worse, I was already twenty minutes late for class – thanks to my dog chewing the guts out of my alarm clock the night before – and as I hurtled down the corridor and rounded the corner, I narrowly missed the janitor, the mop and his bucket of dirty water.

Breathless, I opened the classroom door, caught a disapproving glare from the teacher and sat down.

In a futile attempt to keep the room cool, the windows were open, sending warm gusts of air whispering between the desks to ruffle our papers, to blow them onto the floor, and to keep us sweating: school planning at its finest.

The test was meant to be an hour long but despite my late start, I had finished early – I'm not good at much in school, but math has always come easy. I knew I could leave, but I had nothing better to do so I stayed, taking apart my biro and putting it back together again. Over and over again.

Sitting at his desk, with his glasses perched on the end of his nose, the silver frames glinting in the sunlight, I noticed the teacher's lips moving. It was as if he was in a trance and he seemed to be silently mouthing something to himself.

"Anastasia…"

Who?

"Anastasia…"

Now I may not be the most observant kid in the world, but I have been at this school for over seven years now, and I don't remember ever hearing about anyone called Anastasia. Maybe it was his wife? Or an old girlfriend?

"Anas… tasia…"

The blonde girl sitting next to me, who had been slumped over her desk for the past ten minutes, seemingly dozing in the heat, stirred slowly and looked up as if she was being woken up from a deep sleep.

"An… a… stasia…"

She muttered something under her breath and sighed – I couldn't hear what she said – but then she turned to me and our eyes met.

"An… an... a… stasia."

The emerald green of her eyes collided with the slate grey of mine as the teacher's rolled back in their sockets and he fell to the floor, twitching uncontrollably. From the corner of my eye I could see that he was frothing at the mouth, but captivated by the girl's stare, it didn't occur to me to do anything. Her eyes darted quickly towards the teacher who was now shuddering violently on floor, then back to me again. She smiled, leant forward and spoke in a hushed voice.

"Quick, while he's not looking. What did you get for number six?"

But I barely caught her words. They fell away along with everything else in the room, with the exception of three things: the convulsing body on the floor, the empty biro shell in my hand and the scissors three desks in front of me. I also had a feeling that what I was about to do would probably result in a great deal of unwanted attention for the next few weeks. But I didn't really have a choice.

The morning light trickled through the open windows as I knelt down next to Mr. Davies, and my hand shook slightly as I placed my knee on his chest, steadied myself and drove the scissors into his throat just below his Adam's apple. Hot blood spurted out of the wound over my hands and began to pool lightly on the floor.

Inevitably there were gasps and even some screams from behind me as the curiosity of the more inquisitive students turned to shock, and I heard footsteps approaching rapidly from the hallway in response.

The biro shell slid easily into the open wound, and as I removed the scissors, a violent hissing filled the room as the air rushed into the teacher's lungs. His eyes opened and his arms flailed wildly by his sides as the oxygen reached his brain, so I kept my knee on his chest to hold him down till help arrived – it would only make things worse if he tried to get up.

"Just lay still," I said.

From the corner of my eye I could see the girl perched on my desk, copying the answers from my test paper. She looked up at me and smiled.

The rest of the day was a blur of ambulance sirens, police questions, congratulations from the staff and, as I had expected, a rapidly-spreading rumor that I was a psychopath who had just been waiting for the right opportunity for the past seven years… typical high school!

The next two periods were cancelled due to the hospitalization of our only math teacher, during which time a girl called Anastasia, I later discovered, had taken the opportunity to cheat on a test using my answers.

As usual when classes were cancelled, everyone headed down to the Common Room to drink cheap hot chocolate and chat to each other about… well, whatever people chat about, I suppose.

I didn't bother to go because, having been labeled a psycho so early in the morning, it wasn't hard to guess what the main topic of conversation would be. And I'm not too keen on crowds anyway, so I decided to walk around school for a while, taking advantage of the deserted corridors, enjoying the hollow clicking sound my shoes made on the stone floor and the pale shadows on the walls as the autumn sunlight crept meekly through the windows.

And as I passed the third floor library, there she was.

When you say it like that, I suppose it sounds quite dramatic – like she appeared in front of me in shaft of light, a goddess descending from the clouds. What I really mean is that I found her dancing spastically in the middle of the hallway with her eyes closed, listening to her iPod.

She had her arms over her head, waving madly from side to side as she shuffled from one foot to the other, and there was a look of deep concentration on her face…either that or she was having a seizure and she was in a great deal of pain.

I decided not to disturb her, but as I walked carefully past she managed to trip over her own foot (Seriously? Who does that?) and lunged towards me with her arms out-stretched. Surprised by the sudden movement, I half-caught her as she lost her balance and we both fell to the ground in a tangled mess of arms, legs and iPod wires.

"Hey!" she said, tugging one of the ear-pieces out of her ear.

"What?"

"You're the guy," she said, clambering back up and hopping from foot to foot as if the 'groove' was reluctant to leave her feet.

"The guy?" I said from the floor.

"The pen guy."

"I suppose…"

"They said you saved his life."

"I guess…"

She grinned.

"That makes you a hero. Care to dance?"

I watched her gyrating for a few seconds, then picked myself up from the floor.

"I'll pass thanks."

"Okay," she said, "how about a coffee then? I'm free now."

"Um…"

I knew she was free of course. And she knew I was too. We were both missing the same math class. And those big emeralds were staring at me…

"Oh, come on!" she said, grabbing my arm and dragging me towards the stairs.

———————————

"When you said let's get a coffee," I said, raising my voice to compete with the rock music belting out from the juke box, "I didn't realize you meant we'd be playing pool in the shadiest looking dive in town."

The bar was dark apart from some dim yellowy lights on the wall illuminating a handful of booths, and a large spotlight above the bar itself, making the thickset bartender look like one of the undead.

"Ahh, the world is full of surprises…" she said with a shrug as she sank the white ball for the third time. "I just come here because the coffee's good."

With a flick of her wrist, she threw the chalk across the table and I caught it just before it hit me in the eye.

"Nice reflexes…" she grinned. "Two shots."

I bent down to line up for the corner pocket, trying to make it look like I had played before, but as I did, a tattooed bear with a six inch scar running from his temple to his jaw approached the table and cornered Anastasia.

"Man, I knew it was a mistake to come here..." I muttered to myself, checking the exits and tightening my grip on the pool cue.

He was huge and he towered over her. But for some reason she didn't move – she just kept staring at him. He bent down till his face was level with hers and they held each other's gaze for a moment. I held my breath and I could feel my heart beating in my throat – it was like that scene from King Kong where you think he's going to bite her head off like a jelly baby. But then, without warning, he broke into a big, childish grin – the bear I mean, not the gorilla.

"Here's your coffee Stacy. I added some marshmallows on the side because you're just so sweet."

"Aw, you're too good to me John. Thanks."

But his smile snapped back into a death stare as his gaze turned to me.

"And here's yours," he growled, slamming the cup down on the table and spilling a quarter of it. "Enjoy…"

He disappeared behind the bar before I could say anything. Lucky for him I didn't want a full cup.

Anastasia stirred her coffee and popped a marshmallow into her mouth.

She leaned in and whispered, "Don't worry about John. He's actually really sweet. He just gets nervous around strangers. See? He even forgot to ask us to pay…"

She popped another marshmallow in her mouth.

"Why don't you go over and give him the money? Here's mine. It'll break the ice between you."

She gave me a handful of coins, grinned and waved me off with a gentle shove in the direction of the bar.

The bartender glared at me as I pulled the money from my wallet.

"I forgot to pay… this is for Anastasia's drink…" I said, letting the coins clatter onto the counter, "and this is for mine."

I pushed a five towards him and he snarled, then snatching the money off the counter, he threw it into the cash register and slammed my change so hard into the counter that it practically embedded itself into the wood. I thanked him, ignoring the fact that he hadn't given me enough, and pocketed it.

"How did it go?" enquired Anastasia as I got back to the table, her top lip covered in froth from the coffee

"Just peachy. He's taking me to lunch on Sunday…"

"Aw look, he's blushing," she said. "He's a big softie really. It's not easy from him to act the tough guy all the time, but it's part of the image."

I turned to see him glaring at me with an intensity that could melt stone.

"Hmm, that's odd…" she grinned, "it changes when you turn round."

I turned back to the pool table as she sank eight ball.

"Loser pays for the next game," she said, jumping up and down in delight.

I guess you could say I'd made a friend.

———————————

A week later and the mini heat-wave was over. Stars shivered under the thin skin of daylight waiting impatiently for night, and the clouds glowed orange as the day sighed its last breath.

"Martin…" she said as we lay on the basketball court, looking up at the stars.

"What's up?"

She adjusted the scarf around her neck.

"Six months from now we'll have finished our exams, won't we?"

I ran the dates through my head, even though I really didn't need to: I'd been counting down the days since the end of the summer holidays.

"Yeah, six months from this Friday."

"Half a year…" she sighed, reaching her arms up toward the sky and watching the sunset colors fade between her gloved fingers.

"Just half a year… half a year…"

"… half a year then we're outta here! Oh man, we'd be awesome rappers, wouldn't we?" she laughed.

"The best!" I said. "Jay Z better find a new day job!"

It had only been a week, but we had already become good friends, spending every afternoon together after school.

"Come on," I said, kneeling in front of her and pulling her to a sitting position with her scarf, "Let's head home."

We walked in silence. She was right. Just half a year and it would all be over.

As autumn wore on, the evenings began to get cooler, but the more time we spent together, the less time we wanted to spend with other people, so we'd often go to the park and sit on a wall overlooking the city. It wasn't a very high wall, but the drop on the other side was about ten meters.

Anastasia talked a lot. And I mean a lot. But she talked like most people play pinball, and on this particular day she bounced the conversation from how much she hates school, to gorillas learning sign language, to the number of dimensions that exist, to why she doesn't appreciate Shakespeare, although she claims to understand his popularity.

Normally it's mostly hmmms and aaahs from me, but when she got to Shakespeare I just couldn't contain myself. The fact that he's classified as a genius just rubs me the wrong way. For one thing, his comedies just aren't funny. Sure, they MAY have been at one time. But you're not seriously telling me we haven't found better story-tellers and comedians in the past 400 years? I mean, I GET it. He was popular because he was good. Well... that, and because they didn't have cable back then. But now? Why aren't we studying Robin Williams for comedy? Or Jim Carrey? And what about Spielberg or that guy who did Titanic? Surely they're better story tellers than some guy whose stories are so old you can't even understand what the characters are saying half of the time? It's not entertainment when you have to read a book ABOUT the book to understand what's IN the book. And it's not useful either... how is it going to help us in the future, unless we all have some massive brain fart and start talking in thee's and thou's again? Short answer: it's not. It's not funny, it's not entertaining, it's not useful and it's not education... it's an obsession!

Okay, deep breath, Martin.

As Anastasia babbled and I ranted, the sun gradually turned the sky red, and suddenly, without warning night fell. But it wasn't night. It was just a shadow across the sun: the shadow of a Neanderthal brick shit-house in the form of Trent "Thug" Barker. To say Trent was a bully would be an understatement. Let's just say that he earned his nickname – he was a kid who seemed to have been born angry, and who was determined to take that anger out on everyone and everything in his path.

As a result, having been on the receiving end of several beatings over the years, I had good reason to be afraid of him. But no-one had seen Trent for over a year because he had been "removed" after an incident with the gym teacher – the details were sketchy, but no-one was sorry to see him leave of course, and no-one really cared to ask too many questions… it was enough that he was gone.

Anastasia spotted him and waved.

"Hey, Trent! Over here!"

I felt the blood drain from my face. What the hell was she doing?! Did she want to get us both killed?

As he turned and started to walk over, I considered whether or not I could survive the ten meter drop over the other side of the wall. But I'm scared of heights and just looking over the edge made me feel queasy. My shoulders slumped as I realized my life had come to a close: like the last rays of the setting sun it had slipped though my fingers. It was over. My body (or bits of it) would no doubt be found in a week's time next to that of a short blonde girl, and as my impending doom lumbered closer, step by step, I just hoped that someone would start a rumor that we were brutally murdered while on a date. It would suck to die and for everyone to know you were single.

Trent stood in front of us, breathing heavily through his nose like an angry bull, his brow set in a thick crease.

"Hey Trent! How's it going?!" said Anastasia cheerfully, clearly delusional.

There was a pause. I prayed that he would kill her quickly and not make it too painful. She didn't deserve a slow, drawn-out death.

But remarkably his face blossomed into something resembling a smile.

"Hey Annie!" he said. "How are you?!"

What?! I wasn't sure what was going on, but I felt like I had been transported into a parallel universe. Thug (no-one called him Trent) was a bully with the mental capacity of a rock, a long history of violence and his forearms were thicker than my waist. What I was seeing and hearing now just didn't compute.

Anastasia could see I was nervous.

"Do you two know each other?" she asked.

I looked down, not daring to meet his gaze.

"Hi Martin…" he said sheepishly.

What?! Now I KNEW I was in a parallel universe.

I looked up to see a big grin on his face. Not the "I'm going to hurt you" kind of grin of old, but a genuine smile. I have to admit, I was still very nervous, but something seemed to have changed and he no longer seemed quite so threatening.

"Do you guys want to go to the warehouse? We could sit and talk for a while…"

"Sounds good," grinned Anastasia. "Let's meet up in half an hour. I'll bring the cigarettes and you bring something to drink. And make sure it's something that won't kill us. Your dad puts the drinks in the cabinet, not under the sink. Got it?"

I held my breath. Even the slightest criticism had been known to set him off previously, and if anything was going to turn the new Trent into the old Thug, this was it.

But remarkably, he just laughed.

"Martin, you're coming too aren't you?" he asked.

"Oh, he'll be there…" called Anastasia over her shoulder, making my mind up for me as she disappeared in a cloud of dust and a flash of old sneakers. "Catch you later!"

Trent kept waving even after she disappeared, and then it was just the two of us.

And an awkward silence.

"Well, I guess I'll see you later then…" I said, starting to get down from the wall.

"Stick around, Martin," he said, sitting beside me and putting his hand on my shoulder. His voice had dropped an octave.

Squinting at the city lights slowly coming to life, he pulled out a pack of cigarettes, lit one, drew hard on it and exhaled a long plume of blue smoke. I was beginning to feel nervous again.

"So, how's it going?" I asked, trying to sound nonchalant.

"Don't talk to me like I'm your friend."

The menace seemed to have returned to his voice and the wisps of smoke turned the saliva in the back of my throat sour.

"Look Thu… umm, I mean Trent… I don't want any trouble. Can't we just try to forget about the past? Maybe we can be frien…"

"Unfortunately it's not that easy," he interjected. "And no, we can't be friends… not until I've apologized."

"What?"

"After the thing with Barcroft, the gym teacher, my parents had to agree to send me to a shrink twice a week, or they were going to take me away and put me in a home."

"Wow, I didn't realize it was so serious…" I said, desperate to know what had actually happened, but too frightened to ask.

"Well, he's walking again now, so I suppose that's something..."

I swallowed hard to stifle a whimper.

"Anyway, Dr. Miles – that's the psychiatrist – she's helped me to understand my anger and to come to terms with it. She's very good. And while I can't make up for the all bad things I did, I can at least apologize and explain why I did them."

"Really, there's no need," I said. "You don't have to…"

"I'm gay."

"Oh…"

Silence.

"Are you sure?"

"Yeah, pretty sure. I mean, I'm not one of your "Just Jack" screaming queens and I've never really liked show tunes, but the psychiatrist says I spent years repressing it and that's why I was so angry all the time."

He finished his cigarette and flicked the butt over the wall onto the ground below.

"So, I'm sorry," he said, breathing out the last of the smoke. "And I hope you'll be able to forgive me."

"I had no idea…"

"Yeah, neither did I…"

———————————

Anastasia was half way down a bottle of brandy by the time we got to the warehouse.

"Couldn't wait, huh?" chuckled Trent.

"My dad won't even notice it's gone," she said.

The full moon grinned down at us as broken glass crunched under my shoes and the massive, grey walls of the building soared into the sky.

"Alllllllll-righty then! Here we go!" she squealed, pushing the big metal door with her shoulder.

The building was massive. The warehouse must have been deserted for years and thick piles of dust lay on the concrete floor. A metal railing glinted overhead in the moonlight, filtered through the dirty, almost frosted-looking windows that lined the walls.

Anastasia's feet skittered across the floor as she turned circles, the bottle weighing down her right arm.

"Whhhoaa, this place is so B-I-I-I-G!" she sang, bursting into a fit of giggles.

Trent lit up another cigarette and offered me one.

"No thanks."

"You're right," he said, "it's a dirty habit."

Anastasia placed the bottle on the floor and skipped towards me, kicking up clouds of dust.

"Hey Martin, let's play a game."

"Sure. What do you want to do?"

"I dunno," she said looking a bit puzzled.

She took my hand and dragged me towards the bottle, then danced as if she were in orbit around it before sitting down on the floor. Trent followed in a more sober bee-line and Anastasia indicated for us both to sit down with her.

"How about Monopoly?" she exclaimed enthusiastically.

"Oh no…" muttered Trent.

"Okay…" I said, "but we don't have a board."

"Hmmmmmm…" she said, rolling her eyes around the cavernous warehouse roof, searching for inspiration in the rafters. "I've got it!"

"What?"

"Let's play truth or dare!"

"Um… sure…"

Anastasia leaned towards me as if she was going to tell me a secret. Her long eyelashes swept together in slow motion as she lazily closed her eyes and then – out of nowhere – she kissed me. Her lips were soft like velvet or cream, her breath seemed to condense in my mind, freezing time and the light touch of her nails on my forearm burned like fire on my skin.

She pulled away and swayed a little, tugging at her bottom lip with her teeth, her eyes still closed.

What?

"I'm pretty sure there are more rules to the game than that, Annie," laughed Trent.

I traced the line of my lips absently with my finger. Did it count as a first kiss if she wasn't going to remember it in the morning?

"Well I can't hang around wondering if I've broken a rule or two, can I? What shall we do next?"

And like a hurricane she was onto the next thing.

"What… could… we… do…" she intoned, her head rolling slowly around the room, as if some sort of divine intervention would bleed through the walls and give her the most amazing game idea in existence.

"We could always play spin the bottle," said Trent with a smirk.

Anastasia ignored him.

"Monopoly!" she exclaimed.

"Oh Christ…" mumbled Trent, burying his face in his hands, "not again…"

Anastasia shot him a dirty look.

"Am I missing something?" I asked. "What's the obsession with Monopoly?"

"It's not an obsession," she said seriously, standing unsteadily and spreading her arms out as if she was trying to stop the room moving around her. "Monopoly is the best game in the world."

Her voice shook and slurred with the passion of her words.

"There is nothing better in this world than winning a game of Monopoly, watching the light fade from the eyes of your opponents as you emerge triumphant, a goddess in the world of real estate, the queen of all you survey… it is the BEST feeling!"

"Megalomaniac much…?" mumbled Trent.

"You know that you're corrupt because your only goal is to watch them burn in the economic firestorm that you set for them, but you can't stop yourself buying up land and houses and hotels, laying waste to their dreams of survival. It's all or nothing. Death or glory."

She swept her arms wide, as though she was commanding an army.

"Delusions of grandeur much...?" Trent chuckled under his breath.

"And when the financial tsunami subsides, you sit safely in your multi-million dollar mansion, drinking your fine brandy and surveying the ruins of their lives," she staggered backwards a little as her voice reached a crescendo, "knowing that they will NEVER, ever recover."

"So..." I looked to Trent for support, "we like Monopoly then."

"Yes," he nodded, "we like Monopoly. And that's only one of the reasons we're in therapy, isn't it babe...?"

But she was gone.

"The roof!!" she squealed.

Kicking her legs up behind her, the dust and leaves fell from her hair as she ran towards the metal staircase.

"Come on! The stars are out!"

"Oh! By the way, Trent!" she yelled over her shoulder.

He threw his head back and let his voice echo through the warehouse.

"What?"

"You're part of a club!"

"What?"

"The Half A Year Club!"

"What are you talking about?!"

"Me and Martin made it!"

He turned to me and raised an eyebrow, "Half A Year Club?"

I explained as he finished off his cigarette, stubbed it out on the floor, and lit another.

"Heh, I like it. I've never been in a club before. But now I think about it, it's just six more months for me too… funny how things turn out," he mused.

I didn't really understand what he meant, but I was too concerned about the drunk teenage girl on the roof to ask, so I dusted myself down and made for the stairs to find her.

The aging roof had been eaten away by years of weather and neglect, and through the rusty holes you could see stars blinking in the night sky.

Anastasia was sitting on a thick girder, her legs dangling over the edge.

"Hey," she called with a wave. "You can see the town from here…"

"Come on," sighed Trent as he reached the top of the staircase, "we'd better go get her before she does something crazy."

There was a light breeze and the air was cooler on the roof. Anastasia's golden hair was white in the moonlight, shimmering like a halo around her face. She looked like an angel, and she giggled as she reached her hands out towards the stars and watched them glow between her fingers.

Trent flicked his cigarette butt over the edge and it bounced off the roof a couple of times sending out little showers of orange sparks before disappearing down one of the holes.

"From here the town looks quite beautiful," he sighed.

A sea of lights blazed below us.

I sat between them, Anastasia on my left, still giggling and pinching stars. I wanted to reach out to her, to hold on to her so she didn't fall. Or maybe it was to keep her from floating away.

"Annie…"

"Hmm…?"

"Annie, do you have your phone?" asked Trent. He sounded distracted.

"Sorry honey, my battery's dead…"

"Damn, I left mine at home! Babe, I think we may need to get you to Doctor Miles…"

There was an urgency in his voice now, but Anastasia was humming to herself and didn't seem to hear him.

Doctor? What was he talking about? I thought HE was the one who was seeing the shrink?

Trent was staring at something in the distance and I followed his gaze. There was a large black tower rising up from near the sports field.

"Is that…?" I asked.

"Yeah, it's a fire…" he said with an air of resignation in his voice.

"Where? Can you make it out?"

"My guess would be school," giggled Anastasia, still pinching at the stars.

I squinted to try to make it out through the darkness.

She was right. It was the school.

"Oh Annie," said Trent. "What have you done…?"

excerpt from the novel

Wake Up!

Isabelle Yan

is a high school student in Northern California

I opened my eyes, but it wasn't you.

Where were you? I didn't know what I had been expecting, but it certainly wasn't... this. Two rows of gleaming white teeth floated down towards me, almost blinding in my grogginess.

"Hey," said a voice I didn't like, "so you've finally woken up, Sleeping Beauty."

Wasn't the curse supposed to be lifted with "true love's kiss"? Who was this? I didn't even know this guy... I didn't even *want* to know this guy. How was I supposed to... marry him in a week, according to the prophecy?

"This can't be right," I mumbled.

"Huh? Sorry, didn't catch that. Oh look, the rest of the castle is waking up! Just like it was foretold..." My so-called true love glanced towards the hallway, where some of my servants were rubbing their eyes drowsily.

I had a hundred years. One hundred years that I spent with you, though it was all in a dream. Or was it a dream? You always seemed so real. That day, when you promised we'd be together in the real world...

You were supposed to break the curse. Where *are* you?

Chapter 1

"…I was thinking more of a long train, what do you think? Long trains are in this year. But then you'd trip. Hmm… ooh! Jewelry, we must also consider jewelry! Personally I think you look better with pearls, but your father likes to show off our wealth, as you know, so maybe diamonds it will be. Gosh, I just *love* planning for weddings! I've wanted to plan yours for a lifetime now. And—"

"Mother, I don't even *like* him." I whipped around to face her. She was dragging me down the long hallway to my Fairy Godmother's room to apparently discuss wedding plans. Everywhere I looked, there were tons of spider webs. I guess the servants hadn't gotten to cleaning up all of the hallways yet, what with the castle being dormant for one hundred years. "I mean it, Mom! Like, I am not even *remotely* attracted to him. Are you even listening?"

My mom, Queen Pea, as she is affectionately called by most people in the kingdom, did not look particularly bothered by this. "You know, dearie, in real life, we do not always marry for love. I did not love your father when I married him. Happily ever afters and all that? Tsk, they do not exist in this day and age, dear, not in this day and age."

"Mother, what are you talking about?" I was horrified. "All around our kingdom are princesses being swept off their feet and getting *real* true love's kisses and meeting their knights in shining armor who come riding in on white horses. Why can't I…"

"Claire. Do you really believe those princesses are happy? For all we know they could be complaining to their mothers about their husbands, just like you, right now."

"Husband?" I hissed. "I will *not* marry that blubbering idiot."

My mother arched an eyebrow. "You know it's already been set by the prophecy."

I groaned, and then muttered, "Why, oh why, did you have to anger my Great-Aunt Tilda, who you knew happens to be a Giant Fairy? If you didn't make that mistake, you and Dad, we would not have had this stupid *curse,* and we would not have had this stupid *prophecy.*"

My mother sighed. "Well, we have such a humongous family, Claire, you can't expect me to get along with all of them. I had a tough enough time winning over my mother-in-law, *as you know."*

I snorted. "Look, Mom. I'm getting us off topic. What I'm trying to say is…you can't expect me to marry that guy. At least Dad, according to you, had an ounce of attractiveness."

The story of how Mom married Dad is a well-known one. Did I tell you this story already, while I was still with you? I must have, right? It's been repeated countless times to me, and different sections of our kingdom tell different versions of the story.

Well, just to refresh your memory. According to my mother, one day, she was playing in the meadows with a golden ball, near a well. There was a frog in the well who begged her to kiss him (frogs who are actually princes and need a kiss are commonplace in Mom's home kingdom), but she refused to kiss him and ran away, afraid that the frog would turn out to be some

122

magician who would curse her or something. I mean, I guess it could have happened. She wandered off so much she got terribly lost, and that was when the rainstorm started.

Howling winds drove her to an unfamiliar castle. By then, she was freezing, soaked, and extremely ticked off. She also apparently didn't even look like a princess at this point, being soaked with rain and all. A guard was the first one to see her hovering near the doorstep, and thinking she was a *beggar*. His first instinct was to shoo my mother away. Rain must mess up your vision or something. Thinking fast, my mother blurted out, "I am a princess from Lonia! I have my royal family crest stitched into the back of my dress!"

My grandmother heard her, and the rest is history. My dad the loner hadn't been able to find a girl his mother approved of, and here was this girl who claimed to be a princess! A bajillion mattresses, with a pea under the lowest mattress, were requested for my mother's room. (Princesses are known for sensitivity, but as you know, that's totally untrue in my case.) Lo and behold, my mother could not sleep that night for some reason. She always blamed the uncomfortable and scratchy clothes my grandmother gave her for her lack of shut-eye that night, but a few days later a marriage was arranged. Boom. Prince Frederick finally found a bride! My dad's kingdom breathed a sigh of relief, and the gossip mill ate it up. *What a beautiful story!*

Not.

But getting back to my story…

"Whatever." My mother waved her ring-bedecked hand dismissively. "Personally, I don't think he's that bad-looking. But then again, I'm like 40. I suppose all young boys are attractive to me now." She sighed again. "You'll learn to love him, dear. I did, with your father."

"Sort of, that is." She shrugged apologetically. "It comes with being a princess, Claire."

My mother thought that oaf was attractive? Maybe she needed spectacles. That guy. *Nothing* compared to you. And not just in looks, mind you, *everything* about him was just so… *slimy*. He practically oozed fakeness. I was surprised he didn't leave a gloopy trail when he left the castle (shortly after introducing himself to my parents) to get his parents.

We came to a stop. We were at the door of my Fairy Godmother's room. So far nobody had even given me a chance to explain about you. I was hoping she would listen.

"Come in, Claire, Pea!"

My Fairy Godmother, Merry, is not like the other Fairy Godmothers you may have heard about. For one thing, she's not really *one* person. She's a three-headed dragon. When she was a young Fairy, she tried to perform a Cloning Charm on herself to fight off some ogres, but instead she changed herself into a three-headed dragon. Anyways, it was equally effective, so she defeated the ogres, but she's stuck now as a three-headed dragon, since no one, not even Great Fairies, know how to change a three-headed dragon back into a fairy. I suppose it's never happened before. And technically, I should call her my Fairy *Godmothers*, I guess. Since she's a *three*-headed dragon, she's like three people in one. Shortly after she changed herself into a tri-noggin monster, she decided to name her other heads Flora and Fauna, and they argue with her about everything. Every time I talk to her, I get three opinions.

Yes, that's why I never mentioned her to you. She's really embarrassing. She's my best friend, but she's totally embarrassing. All the other princesses get normal-looking or beautiful Fairy Godmothers, and I get a three-headed dragon. I think I would have eventually told you about her, but it just never came up in those one hundred years...

"So, Claire, Pea told me you guys needed help designing the wedding dress? I still think a shorter train would be safer for you, but Fauna here—"

Fauna spoke up. "Long trains are in this year, Clairey."

Clairey? Ugh, I wish Merry only had one head. Fauna comes up with some pretty obnoxious nicknames. Your nickname for me was much better. *Butterfly.*

"That's exactly what I was saying!" exclaimed my mother. "Long trains are so much more elegant."

"If only you weren't so clumsy!" piped up Flora. "If only you were as graceful as me..." She deliberately arched her head *gracefully.* "Then we wouldn't be worrying about you tripping over if you had a long train."

"Oh, be quiet, both of you," snapped Merry. "Claire, of course, it's your wedding. You should have the final say. What do you think?"

"What I was thinking the entire way here," I said, glaring at my mother, "was that there should be no wedding at all."

"No wedding?" shrieked Flora. She's a big romantic. "You didn't… fall heads over heels in love with the Prince? Geoffrey, I think that was his name…"

"No wedding!" said Fauna, shaking her head. "You ungrateful child, you, Flora and I have been planning all day for your big day…"

"No wedding." Merry looked baffled. "Why?"

I took a deep breath. "I'm in love with someone else." I was referring to you, of course. "There's been some sort of a mistake. That guy. He's not my… true love or whatever. He *can't* be. He's utterly revolting."

There was a long silence. Four pairs of eyes stared at me like I just vomited frogs.

My mother laughed shakily. "That's ridiculous, dearie! What are you talking about. Who could you be in love with? You've been asleep. For one hundred years, along with the rest of us. You haven't met *anyone*."

"Are you running a fever, Claire-o-pear?" Fauna asked worriedly. "Did you swallow too many spiders while sleeping or something? Did you know, actually, that the average human swallows eight spiders in their…"

"…is the guy you're in love with handsomer than Geoffrey?" Flora cut Fauna off dreamily. "Tell me all about him."

Merry was silent. She met my eyes, a concerned look on her face.

"Guys, he's –" I started to say, but…

"I think we need to call the Royal Physician," murmured my mother. "You must be right, Fauna. She's probably burning up or something."

My mother turned to face me. "Go to your bedroom, Claire. You need to get some rest. We need to make sure you're okay before the wedding."

I was now livid. She wasn't even giving me a chance to talk about you. How we fit. How we're supposed to be together. "*Mother, I—*"

"Make her go to her room, Merry," my mother said, and Merry had to listen. My mother's commands are law.

I found myself in my room in an instant. The door was locked and wouldn't budge.

Chapter 2

I was pacing back and forth, wondering what to do. Everything was so messed up. Why hadn't you arrived yet?

The Royal Physician had come by earlier. He deemed my illness to have been caused by, "the stifling blankets piled on me for one hundred years". He made me drink his herbal mixture, which, by the way, tasted like goblin brew.

I must really love you, to endure all this indignations. I closed my eyes and thought back to the last time I saw you.

"You're gonna be there when I wake up, right?"

"Of course." You sounded so confident.

"Good. Because I don't want to marry anyone else."

"You won't have to marry anyone else, Butterfly," you promised. "Alright?"

I gazed up into your hazel eyes. "Alright."

So what happened? Were you delayed or something? Maybe my Great-Aunt Tilda did something again.

Suddenly it hit me like a ton of bricks.

Oh my goodness. That must have been exactly what happened, right? *My Great-Aunt Tilda did something again.* What exactly did my mother do to make Great-Aunt Tilda hate me so much?

Everything was starting to make sense now. I had to find you. Maybe Tilda captured you and she was torturing you and I had to save you so I would be granted my happily ever after.

My eyes popped back open. I was locked in my room, but the windows were open. The Royal Physician had said it'd be a good idea for me to get some fresh air. No one was going to check up on me, because a few minutes ago Lulu, my maid, came to bring me dinner but I pretended to be asleep. Besides, everyone was probably fussing over the wedding, and over that guy, Geoffrey.

Perfect. I would make my escape.

I slung my legs over my enormous bed and put on my "traveling dress", the one I used to wear (before I fell asleep for a hundred years) whenever we visited neighboring kingdoms. The only dresses I had in my hundred-year-long-dream were my ballgown and my weekday dresses (for some reason) so you haven't seen me wear it before.

You should know, then, that my "traveling dress" is quite useful. It's made of this very durable material and Merry put this charm on it that makes it stay clean no matter what I do to it. It's a dark, shimmering green and a cloak is attached to it so I won't get cold or anything (again, princesses are supposed to be sensitive). So far, I had worn it to meet the King of Decalia (and family), the Queen of Maples, the Duke of Nori, and the Prince of Iohly. Now I would wear it to meet Great-Aunt Tilda. *Oh boy.* Wish me luck.

After I had gotten the dress over my head, I plodded over to my shoe selections and laced up the only pair of boots I owned. (Boots are un-princess-ly, according to my mother.) Ack. What else would I need on this trip? Unlike my mother, I was horrible at planning things.

Great-Aunt Tilda reportedly lived in the Lydan Forest. No one knew *exactly* where, but she was supposed to be somewhere in there. So… I could find berries and non-poisonous mushrooms to eat, right? Woodland creatures are supposed to be nice to princesses... I could sleep in tree hollows, maybe... and...

You know what, never mind planning. I stuck my head out the window. I was just going to worry first about getting out of the castle. Hopefully the guards were asleep, but I couldn't be sure.

Chapter 3

There was a twenty-foot drop from my room's window to the ground outside, but I had a secret weapon. That's right. All those blankets that were on my humongous bed? The Royal Physician had made servants carry away most of them, but there were still like six or seven blankets left so I could have a "good night's sleep" or whatever. I could tie them all together to make a rope and climb down to freedom.

It's an old trick, I know, but I obviously had no time to be more creative.

I peeked out my window once more. The guards weren't patrolling the area below my room. So far so good.

As you know, I'm clumsy, so it took me a while to get all those blankets to cooperate with my un-nimble fingers, but in the end, I managed. Then, I flung one end of my "rope" out the window and tied the other end to one of my bedposts. My heart was thumping against my chest. I took a deep breath to steady myself, closing my eyes momentarily. When I opened them, Flora, with Merry and Fauna, of course, was standing in front of me.

I let out a barely muffled scream. *"What are you doing here?"*

"Shhh…" whispered Flora. "Merry and Fauna are asleep." She eyed my blanket rope. "Where are you going?"

"How did you get in here?"

"I used Merry's wand. After years of being stuck with her, I know a few spells. She doesn't know. Don't tell her okay?"

"Flora, why are you…"

She blushed. "Well I wanted to ask you more about the guy you're in love with and stuff."

I told you Flora was a romantic.

"Flora, I met him while I was dreaming."

"And you're convinced that he's real?" Flora's eyes got excited. "I *like* this story."

"Yeah, yeah. And I think Tilda did something to him, so he's late and hasn't arrived yet. He's supposed to be here. I know it. He's my *real* true love." I paused, wondering if I should tell her more. "I'm going out to find him."

She had to use a scaly claw to stifle her squeal of delight. Flora only has control of the four limbs when Merry and Fauna are asleep. Merry has the most authority, and Fauna is second in their little hierarchy. When a dragon only has two arms and two legs but three heads, control of the body apparently is weird.

"I want to help you!"

WHAT? "Flora, if you go along with me, Merry and Fauna will…"

"It's okay," she reassured me. "I know what you're worried about. Pea said that you have to stay in your room, and you think Merry will transport you back to your room the moment she wakes up and realizes you're not where you're supposed to be. But guess what?" She clapped her claws together, ebullient. "Later, Pea told Merry, 'Let's leave Claire alone for a while,' and you know new commands override old ones. So Merry is supposed to leave you alone! Well, for a while, anyways, and then Pea didn't say any commands after that one, so Merry will be free to act of her own accord. Once we're outside of castle walls, Merry won't be able to hear any of Pea's commands, either, so everything's okay! Isn't it *wonderful*?"

I glared at her. "Flora, I don't really need…"

She interrupted again. "Come *on*, Claire. Please, please, please? Besides, having a three-headed dragon fairy with you is going to solve *so* many of your problems when you go out to find him. Haven't you thought about scary creatures, and finding food, and all that? Not to mention your Great-Aunt Tilda! I've heard so much about her…" Flora shuddered.

I tried again. "Flora, I really don't think…"

"Ooh, you're losing this battle, Claire. You know you're going to let me…" she sang gleefully. "Seriously. Like, we won't even need you… blanket thingy if I'm here. I can just murmur a spell and we'll be out of this place!"

Tempting. "*Fine.*"

"Yay!" Flora pulled out Merry's wand, a slender, gleaming mahogany rod. "Ready to go? Oh right. Where exactly *does* Tilda live again? Was it the… Rylold Forest? Er… Lylold Forest…?"

I groaned. "Flora, I'm pretty sure it's the Lydan Forest. Are you sure you know enough magic to get us out of here?" I looked at her doubtfully.

"Trust me!" she insisted, and then reached for my hand. "Three-two-one, *Flowidrian Lydan Forest*!"

Nothing happened.

"Er…." Her face flushed. Red does not look good on iridescent blue cheeks, by the way. I did like it when you blushed though (I realize that sounds pretty weird, but whatever). "Sorry. Um… *Flow… Flowimian… Flownnian…* gosh what was it again? I *just* used this spell, too, to get here…"

I shrugged. "Okay. We go back to Plan A." I gestured towards the blanket rope.

Her eyes grew wide. "But the guards…" She shook the wand violently. "Lemme try again. *Flowidimus Lydan Forest*!"

I gasped. This time, a strong current of wind came out of nowhere and started whirling around us. We were being sucked into a purple tornado. *We were being sucked into a purple tornado!*

"ARE WE GOING TO DIE?" I yelled at Flora. "WHAT HAVE YOU DONE?"

"HOLD ON!" Flora screamed into my ear. *No duh!* I thought, my ear shattered, but gripped the scaly claw more tightly just the same.

In the midst of all the confusion, Merry woke up. *Oh no.* Merry tried to say something… but *wham*! The three-headed dragon and a princess with green, billowing skirts fell from the sky and landed, hard, onto spongy forest ground.

excerpt from the novel

Columbus, Lost in Paradise

Dan Eeds

*lives in the San Francisco Bay Area
with spouse Paula*

Chapter 1
Son of the Admiral of the Ocean Sea

The death cart's stuck and I'm in a devil of a hurry.

Zigzagging my way through morbid gawkers, I see the bodies piled high like marketplace fish, all with gaping mouths and frozen stares. Ay, I hate Sevilla, so-called port city to the New World. I hate its quaint narrow streets; hate its charming three-story apartments; hate its gleaming river. Most of all I hate its hot stench, which today is so foul that horses tremble and grown men faint.

But not me.

There's no time – my father the Admiral likens tardiness to stealing. Crouching like a sprinter, I'm ready to blow pass the stuck death cart and its idiot driver.

Rapido, "Uno, dos – ugh!"

Jostled from behind, I spin about to confront an enormous, grinning mustache. Instantly, hands sweep over my shoulders and down my sleeves. I freeze. The man's face is so close I can taste the raw onions on his breath, and I feel his callused fingers wrapping themselves around my wrists.

Twisting free and fired by panic, I swing wildly. Fists fly and my arms flail like two broken windmill blades. The man ducks and laughs, and as he does, my foot wallops him in the ass. Ha!

He doesn't flinch. And one of his henchmen says, "It's him – the boy, leather shoes and doublet." They all push in for closer inspection, encircling me. I try dodging sideways but get tossed back into their midst.

BOOM, BOOM, BOOM – my heart pounding like a cannonade.

The mustached man proclaims, "The Son of the Admiral," as if he's discovered New World gold. He dares to add, "– only the bastard son, but you'll do."

I'd been warned not to venture out alone on the streets of Sevilla. But testing one's courage requires the risking of life and limb. Stealing apples or swimming naked in the Guadalquivir are mere boys' antics compared to exploring the streets of Sevilla. Better yet, sail the Ocean Sea in a two-masted, 70-foot caravella,

Small Ship + Large Sea = Proof of Courage.

How can one be the hero of his own story without courage?

A woman screams, a dog barks, and from the corner of my eye, movement inside the death cart.

At first the corpses seem very well behaved, silent and still. A man, facedown with rope burns seared into his neck, a thief. And there's a charred slag of ash and bone. Ay, a witch! And a boy, about my own age, maybe thirteen, his stick-legs dangling off the cart, face a grisly terror of jutting tongue and eyes locked in death's stare.

He's died a horrible death, this boy. But there's something about his eyes...

"Que Diablos!" I cry, when those eyes flicker to life and turn on me. The boy sits upright, smiles wickedly and points a bony finger, curling it back in a beckoning gesture that says, *Come join me on the death cart*.

Ay! This is no kind invitation but the Devil's own trick.

The mustached gamberro and his men fall on their knees, mumbling prayers and blessings to each other. Then light as a spirit, the boy drops from the cart and comes at me with out-stretched arms, chanting, "Nanndooo, I've been waiting for you, Nando."

Terror surges through me.

Courage? I concentrate on not pissing myself.

Gulping for air, I try to silence my runaway imagination. *Think of something calming – my little blanket that Father threw in the fire when I was five.*

"Speak ghost," I say.

"I'm no ghost." The boy circles me, looking me over from head-to-toe. He pinches the fabric of my doublet, admiring its Italian fabric in the new trim cut. "I'm just a boy like you."

Like me? He's a wretch. Grain-sack shirt with holes cut for arms and head, a little red cap at a rakish angle. Pants torn-off at the knees. Shoeless. His close-cropped scalp indicates infestation.

It makes me itch to look at him. Street urchin, I'm thinking. Feral boy raised by wolves. I have to ask, "Why did you hide yourself on the death cart?"

"I'm touring," he says. "By the way, those men harassing you? They're an embarrassment to the brotherhood criminals. Their only hope for glory is to be hanged for another man's crime." He spits, as if there's a bad taste in his mouth.

My gut tells me not to trust anyone who steals rides on death carts. "Bueno. Your cart's leaving, you'd better catch it!" The cart's already passing under the Calle Trabajo archway. Also gone, much to my relief, are the mustached man and his gang. No doubt en route to the confessionals of Iglesias de Santa Ana.

But order has not been restored. The boy and I start to circle each other, with me stepping steadily backwards, keeping distance between us. *Maybe there's a knife. No, hunters have knives. A dagger!*

What happens next in these situations?

I say, "Do something – hit me or kiss me." A phrase favored by Father's crewmen and other brawlers. It means, 'You go first.' Pointing down the street to the docks, I say, "What do you want? Can't you see I'm in a hurry? …is it dinero?"

"Dinero?" He smiles crookedly. "I like dinero, especially when it comes from a silk purse."

"No tengo dinero," I say. "Father only gives me enough for the collection plate." Ha! Now he'll lose interest and find someone else to annoy.

"No tengo dinero?" He sighs, and shakes his head. "Are you sure?"

I nod solemnly.

"No problema, I have other business to conduct with Nando," he says.

"How do you know my name?" I demand.

"I know all about you," he says. "But you haven't asked me my name."

"Why would I want your name?" *Time to scare him off.* I choose the famous *en-guarde* fencing stance taught to me by Officer Mendez. The fact that I have no sword temporarily escapes me.

His face lights up, and he says, "You think this is a game?" He lunges, running me through the heart with his own invisible rapier. "Or maybe you want to dance?" He grabs my hand from my chest, winds and twirls me about.

I shove him away. "Idiot! How do you know my name? Tell me, or I'll call for the constable."

"I know his name, Arturo," he says, "mi amigo. He's in his favorite tavern, cool and comfortable, while you, the son of the famous Admiral gets kidnapped and held for a fat ransom. Men – not those idiot men, real gamberros, lop off your ear as proof of abduction. Then they deliver your severed ear to Papa. Si, you need to know the truth. Maybe Papa pays up, maybe he doesn't. Either way, one week later Nando's rotting corpse is discovered floating in the river… hosting many eels."

He's reading my mind!

His brow narrows. "Are you all right, Nando? You're looking pale. Don't worry, I know everyone on Calle de Tino. I will protect you. From the church to the docks, Calle de Tino is my street."

"But this is Calle Trabajo," I point out.

"No longer. I am Tino, the Prince of Calle de Tino."

I want to argue this point, but think better of it. "Ahh, a prince. Why didn't you say so?" Humoring a lunatic is the best tactic, Officer Mendez told me. Play his game, buy myself time until I can spring my own trap. I bow on one knee, eyes properly averted to the cobblestones. "My Prince."

As I cringe in the stench of street urine, waiting for the dagger's plunge, the boy clasps his hands on my shoulders. "This is your lucky day, Nando. Prince Tino is generous to friends, and infamous to enemies. Por favor, you may rise."

"Gracias." I stand. He does have an air about him, more ripe than regal. I can't help myself, mockingly I say, "Forgive me for thinking you were the Prince of Lost Purses." Ugh, why do I do this? One moment I'm in pure terror, and the next I'm an arrogant brat. Shouldn't there be something in between? Goodwill, kindness, loving your neighbor? Now he'll slit my throat.

"Ha!" He laughs, and pretends to write in the palm of his hand, "Prince… of… Lost… Purses." He playfully slaps my cheek. "Me gusta."

He can write? No, he pretends to write. Most grown men can't read or write. Who is this creature? Then it hits me, finally, a small piece of understanding. He wants to impress me.

"Mira!" he says and takes flight, careening up the side of a three-story residence. Without rope or ladder: from street to awning, awning to window bars, window bars to ledge, ledge to windowsill – all the way up to where the windows have no bars, he hangs by his fingers, 20-30 feet above the street. Then he kicks and vanishes through an open window.

It's an impressive display of power and strength. So impressive that a drunkard is inspired to stumble out of his doorway, shouting, "Arriba, siempre arriba." I'm grinning alongside the disheveled man.

But where did he go, the boy? What would he do next? I want to see more of him, revel in his incorrigible spirit. So I wait.

Ten seconds, twenty seconds.

No Tino.

With inexplicable sadness I give up and start down the street. And while still glancing over my shoulder, I tumble over him. Tino's in the middle of the street where he landed in a bare-foot squat, cradling a fresh loaf of pan de horno. With his little red cap snuggly in place, he strokes the bread as if it's precious. I'm seeing this from my upside down, sprawled on my back, perspective.

How did he get ahead of me?

He leans over me, "Half a loaf, Nando?"

The fresh-bake bread radiates warmth and sweetness. I say, "That's stealing."

He reaches for my hand and pulls me to my feet. With a blank face, he says, "The Admiral, does he love you like a son?" Then he tears off a hunk of bread and shoves it in my hand.

"Que? I don't answer questions like that," I say, "especially for strangers." I chomp on the bread, which is delicioso.

"Word in Sevilla says the Admiral is hiring crew," he says.

"We have our crews."

"I'm too young." He's not too young. Almost half of our sailors are under eighteen.

"We have our crews," I repeat, "And too many boys. Have you even sailed before?"

"I have many talents. I can climb anything – rigging, masts, city walls, minarets, and because you are my new friend, Nando… the Admiral will hire me."

"After I make the introduction?" I say.

"*Sí!*" He hugs me.

"Lo siento, there's no chance," I softly push him away.

He bites his lip. His face darkens as if in his mind's eye he sees something terrible, probably his own dismal future. "*Por Favor*, I have a better idea," he says, "they come to me so fast. You hire me, Nando. I'm ready to leave Sevilla, what better way than on one of the Admiral's ships."

"Better than the death cart?" *Ugh, I did it again.* These days, criminals escape the gallows by seeking sanctuary aboard ships bound for the New World. Jews and Muslims excluded, of course.

"You need me, Nando," he says.

"I do? I have a brother – a big brother, a father, mother, uncles, and friends in high places. Why do I need you?"

"I think Nando has no authority to hire Tino."

"I have authority," I say. "I'm the son of the Admiral. And Queen Isabella pays me a handsome salary. I'm her Assistant Keeper of the Fleet Books!"

He gives me a puzzled, one-eyed squint, "What is Assistant Keeper of the Fleet's Books? I'm not familiar with this title. Is he the apprentice admiral?"

"Exactly," I say, "I record all the valuable provisions – food stores, weapons…"

"I can count," he says. "All the way to a one thousand-and-one, beyond that I charge a little extra. I will be your assistant, the Assistant-Assistant Keeper of the Fleet Books. What do you say, Nando? The Admiral has four ships, *La Capitana, Santiago de Palos, La Gallega, and Vizcaina.* That's too much counting, leaving no time for

Nando's important apprentice admiral duties. Am I correct?"

"Can you add?" I have to ask. Most grown men can't perform simple arithmetic.

"Si, I can add," he says. "I'm better at subtracting, if you know what I mean." Shamelessly he blows on his fingertips.

"I believe you," I say.

"Prince Tino at your service, infamous to friends, generous to enemies."

"Shouldn't that be the other way?" I say.

"With Tino you get three for the price of one: an assist-assist bookkeeper, a bodyguard, and, and..."

"And the third?"

"Tu amigo."

"You're hired," I say, But then immediately think, *gran problema.*

Tino kisses both my cheeks and draws the Sign of the Cross on my chest. "I knew I would convince you. Now for our negations."

"Que? Negations?"

"Si. For my wages, Prince Tino, doesn't work for free."

"A real prince doesn't work for wages," I point out. "200 maravedis per month, half the going rate."

"600 is the going rate," he says, "and what is the son of the Admiral paid?"

I hesitate, but can't help not bragging about my own salary. "9,000 maravedis per month. I'm paid by Queen Isabella herself."

"Ay-yi-yi! How much do ship captains earn?"

"10,000 maravedis per month," I say.

"So Nando is the Queen's pet, this is useful information," he says.

"All right, 300 maravedis," I say, countering my own offer.

"Ship captains earn 10,000 per month, and Nando 9,000?" He rubs his chin, "…hmm."

"600!" I say, "600 maravedis, and you must give me something in return. One, you must never call me *The Queen's Pet.* Two, I will be your boss, your patron, you must follow my orders and show me respect."

"You mean make your bed and clean your shoes? I'm a fool to think I can negotiate in good faith with the Assistant Keeper of the Fleet Books. But… I accept your generous offer of… 1,000 maravedis per month."

"Esta bien. Now show me respect, starting now."

He salutes.

"Better," I say. "Now stand straight, tuck in that shirt." He tries to tuck in his shirt but there's not enough of the jute fabric. "I'll find you new shirt – one of mine. Remember this, titles are important around here."

"Bien. What is my title?" he asks.

"Ay! You're a ship's boy. Ship's boys and dogs don't have titles."

"I think Tino must have a title. What about… Prince Tino de la Nave Nino?"

For a moment I pretend to consider this ridiculous title. "Isn't that a big demotion from The Prince of Calle de Tino?"

"True," he sighs. "But the wages are much better!"

"Ay! One more thing, if you fail in your duties, the Admiral will blame me. But you, he will throw over the side of the ship like garbage. ¿Me explicito?"

At that moment I hear the clop of approaching boots. A swordsman, alert and nearly upon us. He whirls, and with one hand on the hilt of his cutlass, he grabs Tino by the nape of his neck with the other and demands, "Who the hell are you?"

"I'm Tino."

Fearing Tino is about to get slashed, I push him aside and say, "Officer Mendez, por favor, let me introduce my assistant, Tino."

"Que diablos! Now I recognize you," the man says. "You're that famous Prince of Calle de Tino."

"You gave me my title last week," Tino says,

"And it's suiting you well." He turns to me with one eyebrow raised, "Your new friend is a fine rascal, and you Nando are late. Half our crew is out searching every church on this side of the river – El Capitana, pronto."

And then the man resumes his stroll up Calle Trabajo, humming to himself a very wicked melody. The one about the knight and the servant girl. This man, Officer Mendez, cuts a fine figure but is otherwise too satisfied with himself. Just twenty-five years old and already he's a senior officer in the Admiral's fleet.

Chapter 3
Ships

Sunrise, morning sounds, sea breeze rippling the river.

Beaching a 50-ton caravella requires: a sandy beach, tide tables, cables and poles, and 15 to 20 shanty-singing sailors.

I try to explain ship careening to Tino, "First we expose her bottom for a good scraping…"

"Que?" He interrupts me, "say again?"

"First we expose her – No!" My face burns with embarrassment. "No importa."

"Por favor, we do what to her what?"

"Silencio!"

The Santiago's hull is thick with barnacles and sea grass. She, the Santiago, smells like low tide itself. I run the flat of my hand over the barnacles, which are hard and sharp, and melded to the hull like a rash on macerated skin. "Careening a ship is the worst job in the world," Father tells me. Then he hands me a scrapping tool and leaves for the Vizcaina.

I feel insignificant standing beside the 70-foot Santiago with my little metal scrapper.

I sulk and watch the barnacles and sea grass fall in greats clumps at Tino's feet. Suddenly, I hear a heavy voice, "Get to work before I break your arm off."

Officer Mendez?

No, it's Porras, captain of the Santiago. One half of the Porras brothers, Francisco and Diego, whom I've come to think of as a snake with two heads. *Humph, obviously he doesn't recognize me as the son of the Admiral.*

Father says the Porras brothers are, 'Useless and vain,'

'Courtiers, not sailors,' is Uncle Barto's judgment.

'Royal bootlickers," says Officer Mendez.

The treasurer of Castile (Morales) hired the Porras brothers for our voyage. Hired them to spy on the Admiral! And it's not even a secret. Officially Francisco Porras is captain of the Santiago, and Diego the fleet treasurer. Neither man can pole a lagoon boat. Why doesn't Queen Isabella put chains on her treasurer? I did ask, but she changed the subject. I was a page in her household. And before that, page for Prince Juan, the Queen's son. The Prince and I hunted together, tutored together, and for his funeral procession, the Queen outfitted me with a little sword and a pony dressed up in green and red bunting. I was only ten on that sad day.

When I said my goodbyes to the Queen, she kissed my forehead and whispered, "Keep an eye on the Porras

Brothers for me. I don't trust them." This tells me that even the Queen answers to someone else.

Tino motions for me. "What's that?" He's pointing at a hole the size of my fingertip, bored into the Santiago's hull. "Look closer, there's something inside," he says.

I shiver and nod. It's white and pulsing, and staring back at me.

"Si, it's alive," Tino says.

Officer Mendez strolls over to have a look. He strokes his black mustache, and says, "Ay, teredo worm."

Teredo worms are found on all fours ships. The Santiago's infestation is the worst. Teredo worms are a kind of shellfish. We try to root them out with fiery torches. Then a ship's carpenter comes along and hammers wooden plugs into the holes. The wound is then sealed with black pitch. As a precaution all four ships are painted stern-to-bow with black tar, a concoction of pine pitch and whale oil. In The Odyssey, it says, '...*the ships' black hulls*.' Two thousand years ago Ulysses' sailors fought the teredo worm.

Tino's discovery has a sobering effect on the old salts, the experienced sailors. Ships like ours, older ships – bargain ships – are more vulnerable to teredo worms. Father says, "No problema, sailors need something to carp about. I have a budget to meet." It's a meager budget. That's why there are so many boys in our crews. But Father has high regard for his boy sailors, who "fearlessly follow my orders."

But this boy sees the hole.

So much depends upon
Four little caravellas:
Santiago, La Capitana, Gallego, Vizcaina,
Riddled with holes.

Tino's one of the fearless boys, I think. He puffs his chest, filling his lungs with the poisonous vapors rising off our tar pots. "*Ahh!*" He peels globs of warm tar from the Santiago's hull and chews it, showing off blackened teeth.

Ugh.

"Stop that," I say. Tino is fearless, yes; follows orders, not so well. I'm starting to think that Tino is a danger to himself and our mission.

The next morning on a favorable tide we refloat our ships.

Tino and I are assigned to ship's inventory, supervised by none other than Diego Porras, fleet treasurer.

But Porras is nowhere to be found. "Asleep with his head between his knees," I suggest. Officer Mendez says, "The man has better things to do than supervise two snot noses."

Mendez warns to keep my opinions to myself.

Taking inventory is the counting and recording of all the ship's provisions. Today the assistant bookkeeper is in charge - that's me. Assisted by the assistant – assistant bookkeeper: Tino. We split duties: Tino counts and I make the quill-and-ink entries in Santiago's inventory journal. "You'll see, Officer Mendez," I say, "two heads are better than one."

"We'll see," he says, and strolls off down the beach to the Vizcaina.

We prove ourselves up to the task. Heavily burdened men, in singles and tandems move up the gangplank carrying cargo. For heavy items such as cannons, a hoist is available.

But then I fall behind in my recording.

"Stop, wait, un momento, por favor!" I shout to the men. The sun rises higher, the day grows hotter, and the men turn deaf ears to my pleas. "Wait! Wait! Stop! Aqui! What's in that crate?"

Officer Mendez passes by and pretends to not notice any problems.

I shout in frustration, "Do something, Tino!"

I'm in a panic. So Tino plays make believe. He's a monkey escaped from its chain. He's walking bent-kneed and screeching. I throw the journal to the ground in disgust. "You're fired!" The loading crew laughs and stops to watch the drama. They're amazed and entertained when Tino performs a handstand.

I pick up the journal and make new entries.

Unsteady at first, Tino walks up the Santiago's gangplank on the palms of his hands. Now all work comes to a stop. One man even attempts his own hand-stand. I'm thinking, it's good that Officer Mendez isn't here to see this breakdown in discipline. The men applaud Tino, and hoot at their fellow crewman.

I keep writing. Tino's antics are working and I'm catching up with my entries. Now he's all the way up on the deck of the Santiago, performing a series of head-over-heels flips, always landing perfectly on the balls of his feet.

Applause-applause. He bows, and goes hands-over-heels down the gangplank like a spinning cart's wheel. But I fall behind again. Now I'm doing two jobs: Tino's and mine! So Tino darts and weaves through the men, pretending to pick their pockets. A rag, a knife, a purse magically appear in his hands. The sailors laugh and kick at him but he is always too quick.

I need to introduce Tino to Queen Isabella.

excerpt from the novel

The Morning After

Myles Gunji-Jardine

is a high school student in Spain

Babel stared at the screen of her mobile phone, wondering how to phrase the message. It was raining outside, which had brought Melancholy knocking on the door with a tub of ice cream and a crappy romantic comedy. And naturally, she had invited him in.

That meant Logic went out of the window, falling face-first onto the cold, hard street below. But he was used to it, so he picked himself up, dusted himself off, and made his way to the bar on the corner.

In the absence of Logic and Clear Thinking (who had gone bowling when she had started gorging herself on the ice-cream), Babel was now regretting that she had recently split up with her idiot ex-boyfriend. The main reason was that the grey, rainy evenings reminded her of the times they had spent together. However, the irony was lost on her – that "dull and miserable" were the two words she most associated with her happiness – so she just sat there, trying to compose something which would send him scurrying back into her arms.

What to say though?

"It's raining and I'm thinking about you. I know this is completely out of the blue, but… do you think we could put the past behind us and try again?"

At least, that's what she wanted to write. But something wouldn't let her. True, she craved his presence. And true, the rain did remind her of him. And she really did want things back the way they had been. But she just couldn't shake the resentment she felt towards him. He had been a real ass. And even if she forgave him, he would still be an ass.

After much deliberation, Babel punched out a single sentence and hit send.

"It's raining and I hate you."

The house was devastated. Bottles lay smashed in the sink, unconscious bodies were strewn around the floor and a nervous seventeen year old was sitting behind a leather sofa in a corner of the expansive living room.

The pungent smell of the leather mingled with the reek of alcohol and sweat, filling his nostrils, and somewhere amid the sea of skin and loose clothes he heard a snort as someone roused briefly before falling back to sleep.

The thought of how his parents would react to what he had done flickered intermittently in the back of his mind like a dodgy neon bar sign, drawing a sickly smile to his lips.

All around him were people he didn't know – strangers who lay passed out on living room floor – and he knew things were never going to be the same again. His parents would never trust him after this. But he could practically *taste* the popularity shift he would experience as a result of hosting the biggest party of the year. He was guaranteed a place with the stars.

Musty morning sunshine strained against the heavy curtains drawn across the windows and bright slivers of light crept through the tiny gaps between the wall and the heavy fabric.

The grandfather clock in the corner of the room released a single chime signaling a quarter to nine.

Not long now…

———————————

Daylight pierced the bedroom gloom and flashed irritatingly across David's eyelids. He screwed his eyes up against the brightness and groaned – it felt as though the sun was doing it on purpose – and he rubbed his left eye with the heel of his palm in a far-from-enthusiastic attempt to face the day.

His throat was dry and his breath tasted stale in his mouth – never a good start to the day. His feet were cold too and he could feel the soft duvet pulled across his stomach, willing him to stay in bed a bit longer.

"Ahh bed, you win…" he said to himself with a grin as he stretched lazily and turned onto his side, hoping to find a cooler part of the pillow but… what was that smell?

Perfume?

Synapses fired, slowly at first, and fragments of the night before began to trickle into his memory. A big house. A party. Laughter, loud music, drinks, flashing lights and…

David took a deep breath and opened his eyes gingerly. Cassie lay next to him, bare shouldered with her head resting on his arm and a delicate smile on her lips. She was wearing too much mascara and her lipstick was smudged, but with her golden hair pooled around her head like a halo, she looked like an angel.

David smiled and took in the view.

"Wake up, sleepy…" he murmured gently, brushing a stray strand of hair from her face with his finger.

Cassie crinkled her nose and sighed contentedly as sleep faded and consciousness slowly began to return. But as she tried to gather her senses and dreams gradually separated from reality, there was a moment of hazy recognition that the voice she had just heard may not have been Harry Styles after all.

She furrowed her brow as she tried to fit the pieces of the puzzle together, but the banging in her head and the sunlight streaming onto her face through the bedroom window made concentration impossible. She sighed again – more out of frustration this time – and as she reluctantly opened her eyes and squinted against the light to focus, she struggled to make sense of what she saw in front of her.

David.

What?!

———————————

Jim heard voices emanating from the kitchen and pried himself out from his protective crevice between the wall and the back of the sofa. Coffee sounded good about now.

From the doorway he could see the Williams twins, stars of the school basketball team, playing catch with a grapefruit; a muscle-bound ape called Chad in a pink shirt sitting at the breakfast bar with his head down, still clutching a beer in his meaty fist; and a tall, skinny kid with glasses whose hair was strategically waxed into something resembling a bird's nest on top of his head, leaning over the stove, trying to light a cigarette without losing his eyebrows.

"I swear to you man," he said blowing smoke towards the ceiling as the cigarette caught light, "hair of the dog is not the way to go. It's a myth. Getting more drunk than you already are will *not* get rid of your hangover."

Chad groaned.

"Dude, you should listen to TJ," said one of the twins, picking up a can of tuna to make the game of catch more interesting. "His mom is a doctor."

"So how do I shake it? My head feels like it's going to explode…"

TJ jerked his head back, flicking his hair away from his eyes and jolting his glasses back up to the bridge of his nose in one deft movement.

"I'm glad you asked," he smiled, sending another plume of smoke billowing into the air. His voice was raspy, as if he'd been smoking since birth.

"First you need to understand the nature of the beast…" he said, reaching for the blender. "A hangover is your body's way of telling you you've done something stupid. It's not trying to punish you though – it's just doing its best to fix the problem you've given it."

He opened the fridge door and took out eggs, orange juice and mayonnaise.

"First of all, you are dehydrated," he continued, pouring the orange juice into the blender. "Your headache is largely the result of your blood being too thick to pass through your veins properly."

"So I just drink water?" asked Chad with his eyes still closed, clearly suffering.

"Ahh, if only it were that simple… no, your body also needs protein too," continued TJ, snatching the tuna from the air and throwing an apple to the twins as a replacement.

"Finally," he said with a flourish as he emptied the contents of the can into the blender and added three eggs, "your body needs some fat to absorb some of the excess alcohol…"

He scooped four large spoons of mayo into the blender and hit the switch.

Chad held his head in his hands, visibly pained by the noise, rocking gently and silently praying for silence.

TJ hit the switch again and finally there was relief.

"And there," he proclaimed proudly as he poured the creamy cocktail into a pint glass, "is the most effective hangover cure you will ever see – a perfect combination of everything your body needs to restore you to your pre-party self. Enjoy!"

He placed the glass on the bar in front of Chad.

"Drink it all up now," he continued, blinking like an owl from behind the rims of his over-sized glasses. "Don't forget, you need to replace the fluids you've lost."

Chad opened his eyes.

"All of it?" he asked weakly.

"All of it," confirmed the knowledgeable owl.

Chad sniffed the concoction and took a nervous sip. And then another.

"Hey, it's not bad…" he said, licking his lips and taking a larger mouthful.

"I'm glad you like it. Drink it all up, and 10 minutes from now you'll be ready to start partying again."

"Awesome!" said Chad as he gulped his way enthusiastically down the glass. "Man, this is going to make you rich some day!"

"Maybe…" replied TJ with a knowing smile, nodding his approval.

"Has it got a name?"

"Sure," he said. "I call it the Rainbow Yawn."

"The what?!"

The twins halted their game and smiled.

"Gentlemen, the door?"

"D-u-u-u-d-e!" they said in unison, opening the door to the garden, then high-fiving TJ and gathering around the breakfast bar to stare at Chad.

"What's wrong with you guys?" said Chad with a puzzled look on his face.

"Nothing, man."

"We just want to see how quickly it works."

When the twins finished each other's sentences like that, it was like watching the same guy talking to himself in the mirror.

"Well I'm feeling pretty good already," smiled Chad. "Is there any left?"

"Whoa there big fella, you don't wanna over-do it now…"

"No, I'm serious," he said, letting out a loud belch.

"That's more like the old Chad…"

"Good to have you back, man!"

"It's good to BE back," he said, with another belch, even bigger than the last one.

"Man," he said, sitting back down, "that stuff really works! What did you call it again?"

There was a look of confusion on his face, as though he was finding it hard to concentrate.

TJ and the twins were smiling. All eyes were on Chad.

"Morning guys," said Jim as he decided to join them instead of watching from the doorway. "What's up?"

"Jim! Cool! You're just in time!"

"Just in time for what?"

"You'll see…"

Chad was pale and beginning to sweat now, and he held his stomach uncomfortably with both hands.

"You should probably go outside now, Chad," advised TJ, helping him to his feet. "You look like you need some fresh air…"

"Oh god…" groaned Chad as he stood up. "I don't feel too well."

"Wait for it…"

"Ohhhh…"

And with a look of sheer panic on his face, one hand holding his stomach, the other clasped to his mouth, Chad bolted for the open door.

"Man, you are pure evil!" chimed the twins in stereo.

"You're too kind," smiled TJ. "Orange juice and mayo is a killer combination, but he'll thank me later… better out than in!"

"Hey Jim!" said one of the twins, picking up the grapefruit again, "Rockin' party, man."

"Yeah, the best we've been to in a long time," said the other, resuming their game of catch.

And with that, somehow the group had opened up and Jim was a part of their world. He was a somebody at last.

———————————————

Cassie buried her face in her hands.

No. No. No. No. No. Not again.

"What the hell are you doing here David?" she whined.

"Well, good morning to you too…" he replied with a smile.

"Answer me… what are you doing here? In this room? With me?"

"You're kidding, right?"

"Do I look like I'm kidding," she answered sarcastically, pulling the duvet up around her chin.

"Well I was thinking how beautiful you looked while you were sleeping…"

"What?!"

"Till you woke up and started shouting at me of course… what's wrong with you?"

"I can't believe it…"

"Jeez Cassie, how much did you have to drink last night? You don't remember the party?"

Cassie looked away. Her head hurt and there were too many holes in her memory to be sure what had happened. Surely this couldn't be happening again.

She looked around the bedroom, the white walls, the varnished floorboards, the tall ceiling... but what was that?

"David..."

"Yeah?"

"Why is my bra hooked on the door handle?"

"That's where you left it... you don't remember that either?"

Cassie sighed dejectedly.

"Would you get it for me, please?"

―――――――――――

"So," said TJ rinsing out the blender, "I saw you with Jennifer last night. Man, she was all *over* you!"

Jim smiled to himself. It was certainly odd, but it was the sort of odd he could get used to. Jennifer Watson had never given him so much as a glance in the three years they had been at school together, but last night she had been putty in his hands. He wasn't interested in her – the fake tan, the false laugh and the complete lack of any personality – but why the sudden change? Jim had always been dismissed as a loser. A loner. A nerd. And it amazed him that one party could reverse all that, and that it could have changed things so dramatically. But change it had – from zero to hero in just 24 hours.

"You'll be needing these," said TJ reaching into his pocket and pulling out his Ray Bans. "Now you're cool, you need to look cool. And nothing says cool like the right pair of shades…"

Jim slipped the sunglasses on and the façade was finally complete.

"How the hell did this happen, David?"

"You really don't remember anything, do you?"

"I… I… remember turning up at the party," said Cassie sheepishly. "And I remember seeing you and avoiding you…"

"And then?"

"And then it all gets a bit hazy… there was loud music… and dancing… and…"

"And too much cheap wine?" he said with a grin.

Cassie shot him a dirty look, but she knew he was right. Seeing him again after spending the entire summer away with her family in Ireland had been a shock and the alcohol had clearly gone straight to her head.

"I just don't know how you could take advantage of me like that."

"What? No, Cassie! What do you think happened here last night? You've got it all wrong."

But she couldn't hear him. Her head was hidden under the duvet and pressed her face into the pillow. Why couldn't she remember anything?

———————————————

"I'll be back in a second," said Jim as he left the kitchen. "I just need to check something."

The silence of sleeping bodies hung heavy in the living room, and as he pulled open the curtains to reveal the full aftermath of the party, the grandfather clock chimed gently in the background.

Nine o'clock.

Jim was relieved to hear the reassuring crackle of gravel against the tires of his parents' car.

Right on time.

Light spilled into the room in rippled waves through the windows, drenching the bodies in a bright froth of sunlight, making them writhe as it hit their sleep-saturated eyelids.

The car door slammed and the sound of footsteps approached.

Standing amidst the bodies in the archway leading to the entrance, the sharp sunlight created distorted shadows on his face. Jim donned his newly-acquired Ray Bans and took his stance facing the door, his arms out-stretched, bare from the waist up, and with his head tilted to one side.

The Pearsons, dressed immaculately as always, opened their front door to the musty stench of sweat, the reek of alcohol and the stale smell of sleep. The muscles in Mr. Pearson's jaw tightened and the lines in his face seemed etched hard into the skin.

Before him stood Jim in a Christ-like pose, the bodies of countless teenagers stirring at his feet, some reaching out to him like an apparition in their semi-conscious state. Suspended on his invisible cross, Jim tilted his head in mock curiosity wearing a crooked smile on his lips, the look on his face straddling victory and despair.

His father speechless, Jim filled the silence.

"So, how was your trip?"

"No-one took advantage of anyone last night, Cassie."

David felt the words catch in his throat as he considered the idea that Cassie might really think him capable of doing something to hurt her.

"Then what am I doing here in bed with you, almost naked?" she said from beneath the duvet, still refusing to look at him. "You know we can't be together."

"That was your decision, not mine," he replied. "You know how much you mean to me and I've thought about nothing but you for the past two months."

Cassie smiled to herself under the duvet. She'd been thinking about him too, though she knew it was wrong. It was against the code.

"Listen, I don't know how much you remember about last night, but you were the one who dragged me in here, you were the one who locked the door, and you were the one who started taking her clothes off."

"And what did you do to stop me?" she protested.

"Stop you? Why would I need to stop you? Two minutes after stripping down to your underwear you were passed out snoring on the bed! I just tucked you in and kissed you good night…"

"Really?" she said, emerging from the duvet.

"Really," replied David. "Listen, I get it. I know you think this is wrong, but it's not. It's right. WE are right. And it's not fair that we should be apart just because your best friend used to be my…"

The buzz of his cell phone on the bedside table cut him short. Sighing, he rolled over, snatched it from beside his keys and swiped the screen.

It's raining and I hate you.

excerpt from the novel

The River

Zachary Nichols

wants to remain an enigma

For as long as he could remember, Shannon Carpenter had wished for only two things: 1) to change his first name and 2) to become a big shot professional poker player. He didn't think he needed to explain his problem with the name, which was given to him to honor his great-grandfather who was some big time World War I hero. But that's like in ancient times, when men could have girl names and didn't have to worry about being cool and all. Shannon also understood that to be a top notch poker player he needed a name that his opponents would respect, like Johnny Moss or Stu Ungar, or with boss initials like T. J Cloutier.

Growing up in the 1980's near the Las Vegas Strip, where all the first class casinos were located, has a way of warping a tenth grader's view of how the world works. To Shannon, there seemed to be only two kinds of people. The heavy hitters who gambled and stayed at the hotels, and the people who served them, like his mom and the parents of every kid he knew at school.

He knew since he was five which side of the track he wanted to walk on. He dressed the part too. His shiny loafers contrasted with his peers' dirty sneakers. His classy dress shirt, top two buttons unhooked, to other's tees. He was big for his age, so he didn't get any crap from his classmates for the way he dressed. And he didn't give a rat's ass what they thought anyways. He looked down on them, knowing that their lives will eventually be devoted to serving him and the other "whales" in the casinos. Getting him his drinks, making up his bed, washing his laundry, cleaning his bathroom. But he figured he'd be good to them. Leave them generous tips, talk to them without making them feel like they were nobody's that they really were. You know, be decent and all.

Shannon practiced every day till midnight, his schoolwork shoved into a few minutes in the mornings before school. He was smart, so he still passed all his classes with C's. His mom couldn't complain – she flunked out in her junior year, when she got pregnant with Shannon.

He eventually hooked up with some dropouts that ran illegal Texas Hold'em poker games, the only game worth playing as far as Shannon was concerned, for minors at an abandoned motel at the edge of the old city boundary. To illuminate the lobby of the motel where all the tables were set up, a hundred battery powered flashlights were bundled together in sets of ten and suspend-ed from the ceiling over the tables. The windows were carefully curtained off with heavy fabric taped at the edges, so as not to leak any light that might make a pass-ing cop get too curious. The tables were circular, about five feet in diameter, and could hold up to six players and a dealer.

Shannon cleaned up most nights. Those kids were no match for his skills. It got so that no one would sit at his table, except for the new fish. And to get them, he had to pay off the bozos that ushered in the newcomers. It was easy money. Their faces and bodies were like open books. Some of them literally shook when they got a good hand, and their faces couldn't hide their excite-ment or disappointment if their life depended on it, and Shannon could pretty much predict what "hole" cards they held. "Hole" cards are the first two cards that are dealt, face down, to each of the players. A smirk was probably a king, queen, or jack high. A bulging of the eye or a rise in the brows indicated an ace high. A purs-ing of the lips, combined with a fleeting grin was defi-nitely a pair.

It didn't matter if he had great cards or crappy ones. Shannon would win either way. If he sensed that another player was holding a good hand, he would raise him at the "flop", the first three community cards that are revealed by the dealer. This would make them think Shannon had a decent hand as well, though he might be holding junk, and would make them second guess how good their own hands were.

There's one thing all these dopes had in common: the desire for a sure thing. Shannon figured out a long ago that there was no such thing, and that the thing to do was to exploit this weakness in others.

At the "turn", the next community card, he would raise them again. If they didn't fold at this point, he knew that they had a pretty solid hand and that they would be willing to go down with it except under great pressure. Or fear.

The "flop", which is the last community card, was what separated the men from the boys. Most of the amateurs who held decent hands would feel that it was too late to fold, even if it was obvious that the "flop" had probably given another player a stronger hand. They were too vested, too emotionally tied to their money on the table and their stomach would hurt at the prospect of losing it. And they would inevitably wind up losing even more.

Shannon, at this point, would be pretty sure who had the best hand. He'd wait, would pass his chance to bet, to see who folded, who stayed, and who placed bets. If a player whom he knew had a better hand passed his chance to bet or placed a timid one, he knew they were unsure of themselves and afraid to risk more, so he would go all-in, which is a poker term for betting everything you've got. Other players can only match your bet, or also go all-in too if they didn't have enough to cover your pile.

They'd fold almost every time. It exceeded their pain threshold because their hand just wasn't a sure thing to them. They just didn't have the balls to risk losing everything. Out of the hundreds of time he did this, he only lost once, to a dumb ass kid who didn't understand the rules and thought he didn't have a choice but to continue.

Shannon enjoyed the notoriety as the big fish among the losers he played with, but it just wasn't good enough. He was certain he could hold his own with the best, and he felt insulted being limited to playing with those he considered adolescent lowlifes.

The World Series of Poker, at the famous Horseshoe Casino, was taking place in a week. The best players in the world would all be there, and Shannon felt he would just die if he couldn't play with those big guns.

So, he made plans.

www.ingramcontent.com/pod-product-compliance
Lightning Source LLC
Chambersburg PA
CBHW072135170626
46813CB00004BA/1575